ORION'S WAR

Ashes of Darkness
Book One

ORION'S WAR

Karin M. Davis

Orion's War logo designed and
© 2025 Karin M. Davis
Cover design by Karin M Davis
Copyright © 2025 Karin M. Davis/DFAM
Publishing
All Rights Reserved

ISBN-13 979-8-9925004-1-7

Dedication

I dedicate this, my first book, to my soul mate, my husband Scott. Thank you for showing me true love is not inconceivable, making sure the rum is never gone, and nothing else matters.

And to Phidget_Kitty:

AUTHOR'S NOTE

This book contains extremely mature themes and is intended for mature readers only. It includes scenes of graphic violence, torture, sexual situations, medical emergencies, and other potentially triggering scenes. It includes multiple scenes of violence involving children. You have been warned.

Disclaimer

This book is a work of fiction. Any similarities to any person or creature are coincidental.

Table Of Contents

Chapter	Page
Prologue	1
1) Of Wolf and Man	7
2) Bleeding Me	19
3) Sweet Child O Mine	58
4) Mother	86
5) We're a Happy Family	97
6) Beautiful With You	104
7) Dr. Feelgood	116
8) Welcome Home	132
9) There Goes My Life	156
10) Should I Stay or Should I Go	171
11) Symphony of Destruction	179
12) I Will Always Love you	200
13) Dark Side	214
14) Brightside	230
15) 2x4	243
16) Raining Blood	255
17) Some Kind of Monster	269
18) Heaven and Hell	274
19) Green Hell	281
20) Invisible Kid	288
21) And Justice for All	291
22) We Will Rise	309
Epilogue	320

My boy finally drifts into a restless sleep as I keep a vigilant watch over the camp from the cramped, iron cage that holds us prisoner. Night after night, I scan for any opportunity to escape. The witch, Sandia Baleen, keeps us just drugged enough to prevent us from shifting but not enough to stop me from healing my boy enough to keep him alive. It has been three long, excruciating months since we were ensnared here, three months since I foolishly let my guard down and chose to trust. Never again.

Sandia Baleen and her accomplice, a rogue known only as The Master, are among the most malevolent beings I have ever encountered in my countless lifetimes. Their cruelty surpasses even that of Jörmungandr, the ancient serpent of destruction. Ultimately, I defeated Jörmungandr, and I find myself equally determined to resist these new tormentors. My hope is that it's not too late for my boy.

Baleen's promises were as hollow as they were cruel. She claimed she would provide us with food, shelter, a community where my pup could thrive, and education as he grew older. She even suggested he might find a family to call his own. But her words were nothing but deceitful fabrications. Our current "shelter" is a cage barely large enough for a German Shepherd puppy. It's so small that my boy, at just two and a half feet tall, cannot stand upright in it. The rogues assigned to our care often forget to feed us or deliberately withhold rations to see the child suffer. When we do receive food, it's woefully inadequate for a growing wolf shifter pup. The only education he is likely to receive here is in the art of survival amidst constant torment.

Instead of the bright future Baleen promised, my boy endures daily "experiments," which would be more accurately described as torture. He faces drugging, beatings, and the constant agony of starvation and isolation. Occasionally, Jameson, the rogue leader who styles himself as The Master, allows his son, Arioch, to "play" with my pup. Arioch's version of play is sadistic even by the harshest standards of the old gods of

Asgard. Baleen's experiments are even more horrific.

Baleen has discovered that my boy possesses remarkable abilities: he can heal other creatures, create fire with his hands, and shift forms even at his tender age of three Earth years. She is also fascinated by his exceptional intelligence for a pup his age. I've instructed him never to reveal that he was born in his wolf form or that I am a Reincarnate. If Baleen knew the full extent of our power, she would use it to fuel her dark magic, drawing strength from the pain of young supernaturals.

My boy's healing abilities have only intensified Baleen's quest for power. Before discovering him, she would torture kidnapped pups or the female offspring from The Master's "breeding program." Now, she has turned most her attention to him. On some days, she slices his skin off to extract his DNA, dousing the wounds with liquid silver to prevent proper healing. She and her colleague, a so-called scientist named Bonfare, then attempt to inject this DNA into the females in the breeding program, hoping to create more pups with my boy's unique powers. Some days, she forces him to heal the pups she tortures, a task that leaves him sobbing himself to sleep, as he did tonight. The only solace is that Baleen sometimes refrains from dosing us with wolfsbane, allowing me a sliver of strength. Tonight, I feel capable of shifting—if only we could escape this cage.

A sudden commotion near the tent where the pregnant captives are held catches my attention. During labor, the females are punished for any noise, yet few can remain silent during the final stages of birth. Muffled cries of pain drift to my ears. I recognize the pattern: a female is likely in labor, and another is trying to muffle her cries. Before we were confined to this cage, my human had been housed among the pregnant females. We've witnessed this scenario before.

Each time a pup is born, the guards and Baleen rush to the tent. If the pup is male, both the pup and the mother are taken to a private tent until the pup turns one year old. In the three months we've been captives, no pups have been taken to these tents. Baleen inspects any female pups and decides their fate: either keeping them for experiments or executing them by crushing their skulls with a clawed hand. The mothers are then given mere minutes to clean themselves before being moved to another tent where they face further abuse at the hands of The Master or privileged guards. The air here is thick with the stench of evil and despair.

Tonight, however, something is different. A female waiting by the tent seizes the opportunity to strike a guard with a cast iron skillet she must have stolen from the kitchen. With the guard unconscious, two other females help a new mother, who has just given birth, out of the tent. One of them approaches our cage.

"Come on, boy," she whispers urgently, "shift, let's go." She opens the door, and I slip out. Straining against the built up wolfsbane levels in our system, I manage to shift into our wolf form. My boy stirs awake, but I maintain control. The females, now in their shifted forms, carry a bundle, presumably the newborn pup. As we race toward the edge of the camp, we are confronted by the guards. The new mother throws the bundle to another female who catches it just before it hits the ground. My boy watches in stunned silence, whispering a bewildered, "What the fuck?" Under normal circumstances, I'd reprimand him for his language, but right now, survival takes precedence.

Just as we reach the camp's border, another female is captured by the guards. Exhaustion and pain are forgotten as we sprint for our lives. The last female runs beside me, the bundle clutched tightly in her mouth. We run, pushing our limits as we try to put as much distance as possible between ourselves and the camp.

Eventually, the female halts, and with a gush of fluid between her hind legs, she shifts back to her human form. "Take her," she says, pointing to the sky. "See the big scooper in the sky?" Her words seem strange, but urgency leaves no room for confusion.

"Ursa Major?" I ask, yelling so she can hear my mind link, recognizing the constellation she refers to. She looks surprised that we understand, but there's no time for explanations.

"Yes, but Polaris," she adds, pointing to the tail end of Ursa Minor. "Run towards Polaris; it will lead you to safety. To the Redwood Pack. My pack. Go, run!"

I nuzzle my snout against her face, take the bundle in my mouth, and sprint toward Polaris, heading north. This is the direction the Moon Goddess herself indicated we should go, too. As we flee, I hear the guards closing in on the brave female who helped us. Northward, we run, driven by hope and the will to escape our nightmare.

Chapter 1
Of Wolf and Man

Beta Jackson

My heart pounds in my chest as I sprint through the dense woods surrounding the Packhouse. Delta Jenny had stormed into the meeting, panic etched on her face. The boys were missing again, but this time, they weren't in their usual hiding spots. Now, I'm racing through the pack land in my wolf form, desperately searching for them.

Alexander and Anthony, the future Alphas of our pack, are only three years old but already notorious for their troublemaking. They are adorable, smart, and sweet, full of boundless energy and mischief. As the sons of my best friend, they're practically my nephews. Their antics are both endearing and exasperating, and though they're a handful, I can't help but feel a deep sense of responsibility for their safety.

I've picked up their scent and followed it across the rickety old bridge that spans the fast-flowing creek cutting through our territory. Lenny, their father, has warned them countless times not to venture to the other side. The bridge is dilapidated, the creek's current is perilous, and the area is frequented by wild animals and rogue wolves. It's far too dangerous for a couple of toddlers who can't yet shift into their wolf forms.

As annoyed as I am with them, my primary concern is their safety. I push on, following their trail until I reach a small clearing. At the far end stands a massive redwood tree. Just as I arrive, I witness a heart-stopping sight: one of the boys—it's impossible to tell which from this distance—falls from the tree, landing on top of his brother.

I quickly use the pack mind link to reach Lenny. "Alpha, I found them. Repeat, I have found them." I can almost sense Lenny's eye roll at my Star Wars reference. Despite the gravity of the situation, the familiar banter helps me stay grounded. I race toward them, my heart in my throat, praying they aren't badly hurt.

When I get closer, I see a tangle of small limbs, arms and legs in awkward positions, mixed with a disturbing amount of blood. Shit. I send another message to Lenny, "Get here with a med team. And tell Jenny to keep Sara away. She doesn't need to see the boys like this."

A roar echoes through the forest, a clear sign of Daddy's anger and worry over his injured sons. As I reach the boys, I see Alex crumpled on top of Tony. Tony lies flat on his back, his limbs spread out and his face contorted in pain with every breath he takes. Alex, the older by five minutes and usually the leader of their little escapades, has one leg bent in a painful angle, his foot wedged under Tony's ribcage. One of Tony's arms is twisted around Alex's head at an unnatural angle, and Alex has a deep cut running down the left side of his face, caked with mud and debris. At least we can still tell them apart.

I shift into human form and begin to untangle the boys. Alex's tiny voice breaks through the pain. "Unca Jax." I shush him gently, thinking he's just hurting. "No, Unca Jax. In woods. Rogues. Near flutterbys." His eyes flutter shut again.

Carefully, I move Alex off Tony and help him sit up against the tree. Tony's breathing is labored, and his arm, once wrapped around Alex's head, is likely broken. I try to comfort him, holding his arm to his torso and patting Alex's chest with my other hand.

"Hey boys," I say softly, brushing Tony's shaggy bangs away from his eyes. "It's okay. Your daddy's on his way with healers, and we'll get you patched up." I wipe a tear from Alex's cheek. "What were you doing up in the tree, little man?"

"We heard sumfin," Alex whimpers. "Den... we... get... lost." Tony adds, speaking slowly as he struggles to breathe through his pain. "Alex, are you sure you saw rogues?" I ask gently, still patting him. Alex nods, confirming his earlier claim. I link with the head of our patrols, instructing them to check the area near the field where Monarch Butterflies rest each year. Rogues can be unpredictable;

sometimes they're lost or searching for food, but other times, they come looking for trouble.

Just as I'm about to climb the tree to investigate myself, Alpha Lenny bursts into the clearing, followed closely by our pack doctor, Doc Hill. I'm not fond of doctors in general, and Doc Hill is particularly unsettling, always seeming a bit too skittish around me. But right now, I'm relieved to see them.

Alpha Leonard

After my Beta Jackson urgently linked me, informing me that he had found my toddler twin sons injured, I race to their location. The medical team follows with the UTVs, but the four-wheeled utility vehicles can't navigate through the dense forest as swiftly as I can in wolf form. As I reach the clearing, Dr. Hill meets me just as I see Jackson, crouched naked, keeping the boys calm.

Dr. Hill tosses a pair of shorts to me after I shifted back into human form, then another pair, nodding toward Jackson. Dr. Hill has always been wary of Jackson, and I couldn't blame him. Jackson Broussard is an imposing figure; standing six feet six inches tall and weighing 260 pounds of solid muscle. He looks like he could crush a person's head with ease. In fact, he has done just that to a few rogues in his time. Though he's not the most articulate or emotionally expressive man, Jackson is still my best friend and Beta.

I toss the shorts toward Jackson as I approached the scene. He quickly put them on, displaying a total lack of modesty. While nudity isn't a big deal in our pack, since we've all seen each other in various states of undress, Jackson could at least cover himself around the boys.

My older twin, Alex, is sitting against the giant redwood in the middle of the clearing, while my younger by five minutes son, Anthony, lies sprawled on the ground. Alex's cheek is bleeding slowly, and his leg is twisted at an unnatural angle. Jackson gives Dr. Hill a wary look as the doctor kneels beside the boys.

"Alex has a cut on his cheek, and I'm pretty sure that leg's busted," Jackson begins, his deep Cajun accent thick with concern as he ignores the doctor's presence. "TBoy's got some busted ribs and a broken arm." Jackson uses his pet name for Tony as he returns to his protective crouch beside the injured twins. His fierce love for my boys is evident, and though he may lack tact, his dedication to their safety is unwavering. When Dr. Hill inadvertently makes Anthony cry out in pain while examining him, Jackson growls defensively at the healer.

"Jax," I rumble, my voice low but firm, "let the man work." Jackson sighs and reluctantly eases his crouch, allowing Dr. Hill to continue his examination as we wait for the rest of the medical team to arrive.

Dr. Hill confirms Jackson's assessment of the injuries just as the team arrives with the necessary medical equipment. The team quickly gets to work, bandaging the boys, immobilizing their fractures, and preparing them for transport. Alex is strapped onto a backboard and secured in the bed of the UTV, while Tony is bandaged, splinted, and seated in the UTV. I sit next to Tony, ensuring I can reach Alex as well.

Jackson hands me the shorts and tells me he'll meet us at the infirmary before shifting into his wolf form and running off. With the boys now in safe hands, I focus on keeping them calm as we head toward the pack's medical facility.

Orion

By the time the clock nears midnight, the boys have finally been patched up: injuries cast, bandages wrapped, and stitches neatly done. I stand guard in their infirmary room in Jackson's body while Lenny takes Luna Sara back to their apartment. Delta Jenny, exhausted, snoozes in a chair beside me, while two vigilant guards keep watch outside. With the recent rogue sighting and the anxiety over the boys' injuries, none of the leadership team dares to leave them alone tonight.

Suddenly, a patrol leader's urgent link jolts me from my thoughts: rogues are once again prowling our territory. This time, they're after a small animal. I wake Jenny and alert the guards before rushing outside. I shift into my red-furred wolf form, feeling the adrenaline surge as I sprint towards the edge of the woods.

Through the trees, I see at least five imposing rogues in pursuit of what appears to be the tiniest wolf shifter I've ever laid eyes on. If the wolf hadn't been clutching what looks like a bundle of rolled-up blankets in its mouth, I might have mistaken it for an ordinary wolf pup. But wild wolves don't carry blankets and clothes, and this one seems to be heading straight for our packhouse. Wild wolves typically avoid shifter packs unless they're tamed by pack members. Moreover, the only scents I detect are those of rogues and my pack, no wild wolves. In my twenty-three years on the Moon Goddess' Earth, I've never encountered a wolf quite like this one. Its fur is an inky black, reminiscent of a starless, moonless night.

The tiny wolf is clearly injured and growing weaker. I quickly mind-link the warriors trailing me, directing them to engage the larger rogues. As I watch, the small wolf veers off course toward a hollowed-out tree, depositing the bundle into the open base before turning to face its pursuers. It bares its teeth and emits a tiny growl. Despite the peril, there's something almost endearing about its bravery. The rogues, fixated on the little wolf, fail to notice my warriors closing in.

I can't fathom why they're so determined to harm such a small creature; it's no more than an omega. What could they possibly want with it?

As two rogues close in, the tiny wolf suddenly stands on its hind legs, its front paws pressing against the side of one rogue. The rogue yelps, writhing and howling as if struck by searing pain, before rolling away and shifting forms. Gamma John quickly apprehends the now-human rogue, binding him with his ever-present zip ties.

The tiny wolf spins just in time to confront another rogue lunging at it. As my warriors engage the remaining rogues in a fierce battle, I instinctively move to shield the small wolf. But to my surprise, it's far from defenseless. I'm quickly becoming drawn to care for this little wolf. Its diminutive size has given it exceptional speed, allowing it to evade the attacks with surprising agility despite its injuries. As the large rogue charges the tiny wolf, it crouches down, rolls over and swipes its claws along the rogue's underside. The rogue howls as blood and intestines slide from the opening the tiny wolf makes. Before the rogue can even process what is happening, the tiny wolf leaps onto its back and bites down at the base of the rogue's skull. I hear a sickening crunch as the large rogue falls, lifeless to the ground in a bloody heap. This sure not an omega.

My warriors swiftly dispatch the remaining rogues with minimal injuries to our pack. One warrior sports a deep gash down his arm that won't stop bleeding and will need stitches. The rest of the injuries are minor and will heal on their own. We all shift back to our human forms, and Gamma John tosses us shorts to cover ourselves.

The tiny wolf remains in a defensive stance in front of the bundle nestled in the hollowed-out tree, its legs trembling under the strain. It's clear the small creature is losing strength, its wounds seeping blood from its side and drips on its maw make his deep black fur sparkle in the moonlight. I move cautiously towards it, hands extended to show I mean no harm. As I draw nearer, I see that the wolf is a young male, with his belly fur matted in blood and the guts of the rogue he killed.

The boy's eyes, filled with a mix of pain and relief, dart around as he sniffs the air. A profound sense of relief washes over his face. Just as the tension leaves his small frame, he shifts back into human form and, with a faint whisper of "dry cow skin," collapses in front of me, unconscious.

Chapter Two
Bleeding Me

Alpha Leonard

I run to where my warriors are fighting just in time to see Jax lean down to pick up a small boy. The boy is naked, with blood covering his torso, dripping from a gash down his side. The spaces between his ribs sink in and each inhalation brings the pits deeper. Dirt, leaves, and debris mark his body, some washing off in the flowing blood, some my giant Beta gently attempts to remove and drop to the ground as he approaches me. The boy's feet are stained black with dirt, and my Luna would have a fit at the state of his little toenails.

My warriors stare in shock at the boy as Jackson grunts at our Gamma, the head warrior, John to grab a bundled blanket in a hole in one of the trees. Jax turns to a rogue who is writhing and howling on the ground in zip ties. "Bring that one to the dungeons. And shut it up, the boy barely touched it."

"What happened here?" I ask Jackson as he begins to head toward the Packhouse with the boy. He turns to me, his eyes glowing. Orion then, not Jax. "He was a wolf, the tiniest wolf shifter I've ever seen. He's so young, though. This is impossible." Orion seems to be in shock as he holds the small boy to him protectively. "Bring him to the infirmary. Let's get him treated, and we'll figure out what's going on from there. John, increase our border patrols so no more rogues get in."

"Already done, Alpha. But, Alpha, Beta... you might want to have this checked out at the infirmary, too." I turn to John to see him opening the bundle Orion told him to grab from the tree. Inside is a tiny pup, its umbilical cord still dripping, pulsing slightly. The baby is still covered in uterine fluids, blood and what might be meconium, the first poop a baby takes.

I take the infant from John, then Orion and I hop into the UTV that is waiting at the edge of the field. The boy was losing a lot of blood already from the look of it and this infant is way too small to survive on its own. Both children need medical care, fast. Even if this boy could shift as my men claimed, he will need help healing from these wounds. And how in Goddess' name could a boy this young have a wolf already? Orion reluctantly lets me take the boy from him to secure him in the backseat of the UTV as he holds the infant. Hoping in the driver's seat, I race as quickly and safely as I can to our infirmary.

Beta Jackson

Halfway to the infirmary, Orion hands control back to me. Doctor Hill and Elder Kyah, our medicine man, wait for us as Lenny skids into the parking space outside the infirmary. The doctor immediately takes the boy from the back of the UTV to the emergency suite and begins checking him over. I hand the infant over to the nurse who is waiting to rush it to the nursery unit. Lenny must have linked the infirmary to expect us. Len and the doctor both listen with shock and skepticism as I describe what I just watched. Elder Kyah, however, seemed less shocked.

"You say he was a small wolf, then shifted to this boy?" Elder Kyah asked, smelling the boy's hair as the doctor starts cleaning his wounds and stitching up the deep gashes along his side that will not heal. I nod, my eyes never leaving Doctor Hill, watching his every move. I cannot explain it, but the instant I saw this tiny shifter, my every instinct switched to protect him with my life. He is connected to me and my future, and I cannot explain why my heart and soul just know this. Nothing in my life has prepared me for this possibility. Couple that with my inherent mistrust of western medicine and doctors, Doc Hill's squirrelly nature and my tiredness of the hour, and I found myself growling at the doc every time he moved.

Elder Kyah pulls a leather pouch out of his satchel. He begins to fill it with various leaves and plant matter. I recognize the scalloped edges of a feverfew leaf, echinacea root, and a flower with five yellow petals I am pretty sure is Saint John's Wort. The rest are lost to me. My Cajun MeeMaw tried to teach me healing plants, but I weren't the best student. The Elder places the pouch under the pup's neck after rubbing it along his forehead.

Even though as wolf shifters we could heal ourselves, and we trusted modern western medicine to help with what our wolves couldn't heal, for vaccinations, and to treat the pups before their wolves came in, our pack was also still deeply rooted in our spirituality and took healing from nature as well. I trusted natural healing far more than I did Dr. Hill and his cronies.

"This will help his wolf heal." Elder Kyah places his hand gently on my arm, waving Alpha Lenny out to the hall as I find myself exiting the room while not wanting to, compelled by the calm resonating from our spiritual healer. "Yes, Alpha, it appears this boy is in fact already able to shift. While exceedingly rare, I have heard of cases where wolves come early, although I must admit, I have never heard of a pup getting their wolf this early. I would like to speak with him when he wakes to help figure out his story."

The doctor remains in the treatment room. Through the open door, I watch as he sutures and cleans the boy's wounds, while his assistant takes a vial of his blood. I hear Doc Hill give instructions to run a blood type on the boy. Joining us in the hall, the doc ignores me to talk to Alpha Lenny.

"He's just lost too much blood for his size. Plus, there's wolfsbane in a few of these larger wounds. I can't even start to close those yet." Explains the doctor, "even an adult shifter might not survive these injuries, Alpha. Hopefully, we have a match for his blood type in our stores." I didn't know this doctor well; he had just recently come to the Redwood Pack from a pack near Berkeley. But, of all the docs we'd had since my family moved to Redwood when I was a young teen, he was both the most competent in his skills, and the one who irritated me the most. "I'll start some fluid to help flush the wolfsbane and hydrate him until the blood results come back, and we just have to hope."

"Wolfsbane... not too many wolves out there that use wolfsbane to fight other wolves." I growl, angry at the tactic. Wolfsbane is poisonous to wolf shifters, even worse than it affects humans. It stops us from shifting to our wolves, slows or prevents healing, and weakens even the strongest wolf. Enough could even kill us. It is the only thing besides silver we're truly susceptible to. It was a well-known but frowned upon tactic to paint one's claws with a wolfsbane solution to cause further injury to your opponent in battle. In fact, it was outlawed by the Lycan Council in 1949, when the leaders of multiple packs and other super naturals that had been involved in World War Two held a Supernatural Geneva Convention of sorts. Even then, some rogues and other dirty fighters still use the tactic.

"They were rogues. You know whose rogues fight like this, Alpha?" I know Leonard understands what group I am talking about. We had been hunting them down for 3 years, ever since their leader, a sadistic predator who called himself the "Master" murdered my sister. "I was thinking the same" Leonard replies grimly.

Doctor Hill looks over at me; I swear he is the world's most nervous doctor around me, "uh, if you'll excuse me Alpha, Beta, I would like to go check on the infant you found with him. The midwife is with the baby now."

"Of course, we will come with you" I walk back into the boy's room as my Alpha tells the squirrel doctor we will accompany him. When I don't move from the boy, instead holding his tiny hand, Leonard eyes soften. "What's going on, brother?" Leonard is my best friend, but this is the first time I can't find the words to answer him. This is the first time he has ever seen the tears that were now falling from my eyes, even when he told me of my sister's murder at the hands of the brutal rogue leader. I can't explain why, but I felt an overwhelming need to protect this little boy. "I need to stay with him, Lenny. I can't explain why, but something is drawing me to this kid. I just can't leave him alone. It's like the Goddess herself is commanding me and my wolf to protect him."

Cocking his head to the side, Leonard pat my shoulder, "stay with him, Bro. He'll need a friendly face when he wakes up, anyway. You can also make sure he's not a security risk to the Pack, if he's such a badass little fighter like you said," Lenny laughs, still not so sure about what I said this little guy could do.

I follow the doctor into the nursery, my thoughts swirling like a storm. Inside, Melissa, my wife's best friend and our pack's midwife, is bent over the infant found with the mysterious boy. She moves with careful precision, her hands steady but her eyes shadowed with worry. The boy is a puzzle I can't stop trying to piece together. Where did he come from? How did he end up with a newborn? Were they abandoned by their parents? And why were rogues hunting them?

But the most baffling question of all—how could such a young pup shift, let alone fight with the skill Jackson described? He was barely a toddler, yet he'd managed to hold his own against grown wolves. I have to find the answers. As Alpha, it's my duty to protect my pack, but it's also my responsibility to shield the innocent. And there's no one more innocent than a newborn.

The baby will need us, our care, our protection, and if we can, we'll reunite her with her mother. Assuming, of course, we can figure out who her mother is. As for the boy, his innocence is still uncertain. That's why I left Jax with him, to keep watch and make sure there's no hidden danger in him that we haven't seen yet.

"Alpha Leonard, good morning," Melissa greets me as I step into the nursery. Her voice is warm, but there's tension beneath it. She looks up from the infant, her usually bright expression subdued.

"Good morning, Melissa." I offer her a small smile, though it's hard to summon much cheer under the circumstances.

"How's my Sara doing?" Melissa asks with a fond smile, but it fades quickly.

"She's glowing, as always," I reply.

"I wasn't expecting to see you here at this hour, though. What brings you in so early?"

"I had to check in on the little one," I admit, gesturing toward the baby. I pull her into a quick hug; Melissa is like family; someone I've known since we were pups ourselves. But when I glance back at the baby, my chest tightens. "How's this one doing?"

Melissa's face falls, and I feel the weight of her worry hit me like a punch.

"She's a fighter, Alpha," Melissa says softly. "But it's not good. She's premature, probably about four weeks early. Honestly, I'm not sure how she's even survived this long without an incubator. It's a miracle she's alive at all." She exhales shakily, brushing a tear from the corner of her eye. "Her heart and lungs are underdeveloped, and I doubt her mother had any prenatal care or proper nutrition during the pregnancy. We've got her on oxygen and formula, but it's going to be touch and go. She's so tiny... so fragile."

Her voice wavers, and I see tears glistening in her eyes. Melissa, one of the toughest wolves I know, is on the brink of breaking down. And I can't blame her.

I glance at the infant, her tiny chest rising and falling with labored breaths, and my heart clenches. She looks impossibly small, swaddled in the sterile white of the infirmary blanket. A fighter, Melissa said. And she'll have to keep fighting if she's going to make it.

"I'll do whatever it takes to make sure she has that chance," I promise, my voice low but firm.

Melissa nods, her composure slipping for just a moment as she presses her lips together tightly.

And then there's the boy, this enigma who managed to protect her long enough to get her here. I've never felt so shaken. Not by the rogues. Not by the danger. But by these two children who've somehow found their way into our care.

I've seen Jackson stand unshaken against the strongest threats, and I've never seen Melissa falter under pressure. But tonight, they both cried. Over these two pups.

And now, standing here, looking at this tiny, fragile life and thinking about the boy's impossible strength, I understand why.

I let Melissa tell the Alpha what was going on with the infant. She is much more of an expert with neonate pups than I, and I am exhausted from working on the boy and the Alpha pups earlier. After I listen to Melissa, I excuse myself and head to my office to write some patient charts. One of the nurses comes in and hands me the report on the boy's blood type. Oh, man. This is not good. I've only seen this blood type once before. It's going to be impossible to find a donor for this boy and without shifter blood the pup will die. And with Beta Jackson's level of concern for the boy, I am actually afraid he might blame me and come after me if the boy doesn't survive. I walk down the hallway to the waiting room, where I found the Alpha getting a coffee from the Keurig. I guess he realized his night was shot, too.

"Alpha, we have a problem" Leonard looks at me sharply and raises his eyebrow for me to continue. "The boy has an extremely rare blood type. So, rare that I've only ever encountered it once, and the she wolf was already dead. Unless we can find a first order relative, we are most likely going to lose the boy."

"Speak English, Doc, we're not but humble werewolves" Beta Jackson grumbled from the doorway, startling me. I knew Beta didn't trust me yet, but the previous doctor had warned me he didn't trust doctors at all, after a medical error contributed to the loss of his parents when he was a child. "Well, Beta, to put it simply, we need to find his mother, father, or a sibling to have the best chance of a blood match. He has O- blood, with wolf A and C antigens. Only an exact match can donate blood to him. I've only seen it once in my career, and it was during an autopsy three years ago at the Berkeley Pack."

Jackson slowly raises his head to look at me, taking a deep breath. "Whose autopsy?" he demands gruffly, grabbing my overcoat and lifting me off the floor. "Uh, th.. th..the Beta's mate. The young woman was kidnapped and murdered on her way to join our pack ..." Beta Jackson cuts me off with a loud roar and drops me into a heap on the floor.

"Shit," Alpha Leonard mutters quietly as Jackson storms down the hall, knocking over computer workstations and other things stored in the hall on his way. "That she wolf was his twin sister" He finishes softly as he follows his Beta down the hall.

Stunned, I pick myself up and follow the men. I find them at the chairs for family members outside the young boy's room. "Do you think he could be Katrina's pup?" Jackson asks Leonard softly. "Maybe, Bro. We know her and Kade were seeing each other before he was killed, then she went to that ballgame, and found her mate from the Berkeley Pack." "But, a pup, man? She would have told me, wouldn't she?" "I don't know, man. She was being so secretive after Kade..."

"Um, excuse me, Beta, I am sorry. I didn't know Lady Katrina was your sister. H...H... However, as twins, there's a good chance you may have the same blood type as Lady Katrina, meaning you could have the same as the boy! It's not guaranteed, since you're obviously not identical twins, but it may be our best chance." Beta was known for his temper, some said he was even stronger than our Alpha, and with his dislike of doctors, he always made me nervous. Here I am, one of the first wolf shifters to have both a medical degree from Stanford and a veterinary degree from UC Davis, published in both human and supernatural medical journals and I am scared shitless of this Beta. And now his wolf is glaring at me, Beta's eyes glowing, letting me know his wolf is about to take control "If, if we could just run a quick test, we could see if yo... you ma.. ma.. ma.."

"Enough!" Jackson roars, the glow dimming in his eyes letting me know the man has taken control of his body back. "Damn it, Doc! I'm only going to kill you if the boy dies! Grow a pair, Man! Test me, for fuck's sake!" I swear I saw the Alpha smirk a little, but it still didn't calm my nerves one bit. We walk over to the lab area, where I am dismayed to find the nurse who normally did the blood draws was off for the evening. Damn it. I'd have to draw Beta's blood myself. I had taken blood and done dental work on non-sedated alligators, wolves, and tigers during my veterinary internship at the Audubon, but I am scared to death of taking a simple sample from Jackson.

Doctor Hill, we have a problem with one of the warriors. He tore his stitches and is still bleeding. The nurse that had been helping the warrior injured in the battle mind-linked me. *YES! I mean, um.. okay, I'll be right there. Can you send someone to come draw a blood sample on Beta Jackson in the lab, I need to do a blood type and match on him to see if he matches the young boy that was brought in. Thank you.* I mind-link back. I shouldn't be happy one of my patients is bleeding, but, fuck, I do not want to stick a needle in that man. I explain, mostly to the Alpha, what was going on and practically run down the hall. Maybe I did need to grow a pair.

Beta Jackson

Doctor Hill tells Lenny another patient needs him and runs out of the lab down the hall like a bat outta hell. I seriously do not know why that man is so afraid of me, but it is funny as fuck, so I play into it. I mean, I still don't trust him, but there's no reason for the straight terror. My wolf starts going nuts in my head as I hear muffled footsteps coming down the hall. *Do you smell that?* He starts jumping around like a puppy. *What the hell, Orion, calm down!* I don't need to be distracted by my wolf going nuts right now, I need to think about this situation with the boy. Especially if he might be Katrina's son. Katrina was my only close family after our parents died. Rogues had taken my parents, my friend Kade, then her, and if this boy was hers, I damned sure wasn't going to let him be lost to them, too.

Lost in my thoughts about the tiny wolf boy, I am hit by the most wonderful smell of spiced rum and strawberry. *Mate! It's Mate! She smells like those drinks we had last time we saw MeeMaw.* Orion roars in my head. *Dude, calm down. I smell it, too, but we must help the boy. If she's really our mate, she'll understand.* Orion grumbled but understood. It weren't a nurse that walked in, though, at least not from what she is wearing. She is gorgeous. I look into her eyes as she looks at me with a shocked expression.

"Mate" we both say at once. Leonard stands there grinning at us like a fool.

"Well, tonight just gets more and more interesting" Leonard starts chuckling. "Melissa, meet Jackson, my Beta. Jackson, this is Melissa, Pack's midwife, and Sara's best friend. Kind of surprised you two haven't ran into each other yet."

"Hello," gently taking her hand and pulling her toward me, I plant a soft kiss on her forehead and smell her again. That may sound a little creepy, but for wolf shifters, our mate's scent is calming, and at this moment, I really need some calming. "I really want to get to know you better, but there's a little boy dying down the hall who my blood might save. Apparently, the doc needs a sample drawn for testing."

Melissa shook her head, then nods slowly; she seems slightly nervous. "Of course, that's why I came down here anyway. The nurses are helping Doctor Hill with a warrior and, well, we really do need to talk before you decide to accept me" *What, of course we are going to accept her! What the hell does she mean, Jax? Mark her, mark Mate NOW!* Orion roared and tried to take over. I struggled, but got him under control *Damnit, calm down, we will not mark her without her consent! And of course we will accept the Goddess' gift. Now shut up, Orion.*

"Whatever you say, I will accept you, *mon petite chère*," I assure her as she gathers the supplies to draw my blood. I look around the room, but Lenny has suddenly disappeared. "I promise, whatever it is you are worried about, I can handle." I smile at her as she swiftly draws my blood. Damn, she's good at that, I didn't even feel it. Either that, or I can't tell over the sparks I feel every time she touches me. Now I know why Lenny and Sara disappeared for a week when they met each other four years ago. I can't take my eyes off her.

Melissa smiles at me as she placed the vial in a bag and places it in a little cubby in the wall. "It takes about 30 minutes to run the test. After that, Dr. Hill will know whether you can be a donor for the boy. Has he woken up yet? Has he said anything? I wondered if he knew anything about the little girl that he was carrying?"

"No. He passed out as soon as he saw me. Wait! He did say 'dried cow skin', but I have no idea what that means." I tell her. I really wanted to spend time with her, but I was also drawn to the boy. Something was telling me I need to protect him. "Would you like to come with me to see him?"

"I'd love that" Melissa smiles at me again. Before we leave the little room she had drawn my blood in, I lean in and kiss her gently on the lips. "I know most mates move a bit faster, but I really need to be here for this boy, too, *mon petite chère*. I hope you don't mind" I never beg, but I'm so torn between my boy and my mate right now, begging is about all I can do. "Not at all, I feel like the Moon Goddess needs us both in this infirmary tonight. I was not even on tonight; I was doing some research when they brought the baby in. It was fate that brought us both here tonight and I think we're supposed to stay awhile." She pauses to smile at me. She sniffs me, then opens her eyes wide and chuckles at me.

"What's funny?" I ask, worried now.

"I just wonder, did the boy mean leather?"

"Huh?"

"Dried cow skin. You said he said that before he passed out. I wonder if he means leather... because that's what you smell like. Leather and rum. Maybe you smell like leather to him, too?" Wow. She thought I smelled like rum, too. I guess we have that in common. For wolf shifters, our mates are said to smell like our favorite scents. For me, strawberries and spiced rum. I have a thing for strawberry daiquiris. I know, fruity drinks are not really considered "manly", but I went to college at Louisiana State University and daiquiris are huge in Southern Louisiana, so they really grew on me until they became a favorite, next to just plain ol' rum and cola. And she likes the smell of rum, too. *Mate's so pretty and smells so good.* Orion is practically purring in my head.

"Jackson?" Shoot, I totally spaced out looking at her. I am not sure what she just asked me. I look at her with a sheepish smile, "sorry, I kind of spaced off, what were you saying?"

"I was wondering if the boy was smelling your scent. Like, your more individual scent, not just as a wolf shifter." We could tell someone was a wolf shifter, rogue, human, and even what pack they were from by their scent, but more individualized scents, like her delicious strawberry rum combination, it was said only family, mates or very close friends could detect.

"Well, his blood type is the same as my twin sister's; we're wondering if he may be related to me." We reach his room and I motion for her to enter before me. The little guy is still passed out, only a sheet covering his lower body. His larger wounds are bandaged, but he still looks rough, covered in bruises and scratches that are healing too slow. I'd seen warriors come out of battles looking less rough. It made my soul hurt to see such a small child so badly hurt, especially one I was beginning to think was my nephew.

"He's adorable." Melissa whispers as she gazes at him. "What could rogues have wanted with him so badly they would do this to him? Some of these injuries are old, they didn't happen just tonight."

"I don't know, Melissa." I reply, noticing the tears in her eyes. *Mate's crying, kiss her, make her better.* Orion whimpers, not able to stand seeing his mate hurting, physically or emotionally. *I get it, Ry, we will help her. She's sad because our new little friend is hurt.* I reach out and take Melissa into my arms as we stand by the side of the boy's bed, watching his little chest rise and fall in slow shaky breaths. *Little pup smells like Kat.* Orion mentions. *Gotta fix little pup.* Kat was my sister's wolf's name. *Kat or a cat, feline type, Ry?* Orion likes kittens, so he really could be talking about either. Most wolves have much different names than their human counterparts, but Katrina's wolf was named Kat. All I can smell from the boy was blood and wolfsbane, and the dirty scent of rogues on him, but Orion could pick up more scents than I could myself. I can tell he doesn't smell like a rogue, though, their foul scent is just on him.

We stand there watching him sleep in silence for a while. Eventually, I sit down in the chair, bringing Melissa with me. As we watch him, his breathing starts to get faster and he begins to whimper. It looked like he was having a nightmare.

"Nnnoo, Master... I won't... I not a bad pup. No... don't make me." The boy starts crying out in his sleep. His rough movements start to rip the stitches the doc put in. I instinctively reach out to hold him, as Melissa rose to hold his hand as well. I place my hand on his forehead, hoping to calm him. His eyes snap open and he looks around in fear.

"It's okay, Buddy. You're safe." I gently look at him while I rub his head, hoping to calm him so he won't be scared. He looks up at me and relief visibly washes over his little body. As he relaxes and closes his eyes, he rolls the side of his head against my hand and whispers, "Red wolf, dry cow skin, you keep me safe" and falls back asleep. I look at Melissa as she stares at my hair. My red hair, which matches my wolf's fur. "He knows you?"

As Melissa stares at me, Doc Hill bursts into the room, his eyes sparkling, his mouth turned upward, happier than I've ever seen the man. His smile falters as he looks at us.

"What's wrong?" He immediately goes to the pup's side and starts looking him over. A crumpled piece of paper clutched in his hand, his eyes dart over to the machine connected to the red, white and black wires stuck to his tiny chest.

"He had a nightmare and woke up briefly, Doc. He's back asleep, though." I say, breaking my stare at Melissa. "What's that?" I point at the paper in his hand. Doc's smile returns as he looks at me.

"You're a match! A perfect match, in fact. All your markers and the boy's are the same. We can start a transfusion whenever you're ready, the sooner the better."

"Let's do it. This boy trusts me, I will do whatever it takes to help him." I don't trust modern medicine, but I trust this doctor to help me help this little guy, especially if I want the mystery about who he is solved.

"I'll get things set up" Melissa pecks my cheek with a light kiss. Doc cocks his head as he watches her stand from my lap and head out of the room.

"I didn't know you and Miss Melissa were close." Doc poorly tries to hide a smile. I shrug and he points to the chair I'm in. "Those things are horrible for shifters. Beta, I'll get a bed brought in here. You'll need to rest after we take the blood from you. He's going to need at least two or three pints, but I can't let you donate more than one pint every 12 hours, so it will be a slow process." I glare at him.

"Doc, I'm huge, surely you can take more than a pint of blood at a time. I lose more than that in battle and am fine!" my wolf and I can't tolerate the thought of delays to the boy getting better.

"We might be able to take two pints at once, but it will make you very weak."

"I don't care, DO IT!" I command him. As a Beta, I have the power to compel him, and anyone in our pack except Alpha Leonard, Luna Sara, and their boys, to obey any orders I give if I force my aura into the command. I hate doing it unless I have to though, preferring to allow pack members the curtesy of choice. But after his nightmare and what he said, I can't wait longer than necessary to get the pup better.

"Yes, Beta." Doctor Hill responds automatically, bowing his head in submission as he does. I shove the chair out of the way as a nurse brings in an adult size bed and sets it next to the pediatric bed the boy sleeps in. Melissa returns with a blue cart that looks like a large, wheeled tool chest. It has two machines on top. Doctor Hill explains how one will take the blood from me and filter out any impurities in my blood, like alcohol or medicines. I don't have any of that in my system but decide not to argue. That machine also puts the blood into a bag that is loaded into the next machine to infuse it into the boy at a controlled rate. The cart is full of the supplies they need to do this, along with medications the doc said in case I pass out, the boy gets sick from my blood or something else happens.

Melissa pushes me onto the bed, saying it will be easier if I was there already if I faint later. Well, she tries to push me into the bed. She has no success until I give in and let her. A nurse hooks up an IV and my blood starts running into the first machine. It takes about 15 minutes, and the first bag is full.

"How are you feeling?" Melissa asks me, I could tell she was concerned about hooking up the next bag. "I'm fine" I ain't lying, I feel fine. "Let's just get this blood for the little guy. I'll be okay". Melissa looks skeptical, but she sets the machine to start taking a second pint of my blood anyway. Doctor Hill starts the first pint of blood into the boy. "Now, we just hope this helps and he doesn't have a bad reaction." Doctor Hill tries to smile at me and Melissa, but I can tell he was still nervous. He starts removing the bandages from the boy's larger wounds. "I want to be able to see if it's helping him heal, too." The doc explains. Streaks of red jet out from the boy's wounds. I hope he ain't getting an infection. Who knows what he could have gotten in those cuts running through the woods?

As the second pint of my blood was drains into the machine, I started feeling tired. I know it is probably from blood loss, but I convince myself I am just tired from the long night. When the second pint is done, Doctor Hill says he wants to wait to take any more blood from me. I am getting pale he claims. I refuse to stop until they have the three pints the doc said my boy needs.

"We're still putting the first pint into him, Beta. Your breathing is getting rapid, and your skin is pale and cold. If we take any more blood, you'll go into shock. We won't even need a third pint for several hours. If we even do." I am on the verge of ordering him to take my blood when Alpha Leonard walked in.

"What's going on?" Lenny looks directly at me when asking.

"They are taking my blood for the boy, but the doc wants to stop for a while.

I'm fine though. The boy needs it" I answer him, hoping he'll take my side. Leonard looks over at the bag of my blood waiting to be loaded into the machine that was infusing the first bag into the boy.

"Well, I agree with Doc. You look like shit, bro. No arguing. You're no good to me, the pack, or the boy if you're unconscious." He had a point, I guess. Melissa guides me to lay back on the bed and smiles at Leonard. Her eyes go hazy as she talks to someone over the mind-link. Len smiles and pats her shoulder as he walks toward the boy. I can't help the low growl that escapes me when he touches her. "Seriously, Jax? I am mated, to your Luna. Besides, I've known Melissa since we were pups, even longer than I've known you or Sara. Chill bro" Len chuckles at me and playfully punches my shoulder. He knows how possessive our wolves can get of our mates, especially before marking. Fucker is highly amused by me finally finding my mate.

I walk into the boy's room, the atmosphere tense. Jax looks pale as fuck but is arguing with Doctor Hill. I end the argument by telling Jax I agree with the doctor.

Thank you, Alpha Melissa mind-links me *He's a stubborn one, I guess.*

Just protective. He's like this with the twins, too. Wait until he's protective of you. I replied, patting her shoulder as I look at the kid. Jackson growled at me when I touched her. *See.* I link again, chuckling at my friend as I punch him in the shoulder. Melissa and I have known each other since we were pups; she has been my mate's best friend since elementary school. It is totally normal for male wolves, and even females, to be possessive of their mates, but it is still funny to me. Jax deserves some happiness in his life, and I am sure Melissa will bring him some.

I look at the boy. He is still sleeping, but it seems like some of the smaller cuts are starting to heal. Jax's wolf shifter healing properties in his blood must be helping the little guy. The larger gashes on his side are taking longer to heal, likely from the wolfsbane. The pup will probably have scars from those for the rest of his life.

"Doctor Hill, is there any way the wolfsbane can be washed out of those gashes? Maybe help them heal faster?" I know wounds are often cleared to help them heal. Just earlier, Jax cleaned Alex's face wound to facilitate healing. I wonder if it would work on wolfsbane, too.

"We can, I just want him more stable before we wash out the wounds. He may start bleeding again and he can't lose any more." Well, that made sense.

"Okay, keep me updated." I turn to Jackson, "Let me know how things are going here. I've got to check in on my boys, then go see Sara at the pack house." I point at Jax "No more blood donating until the doc says it's safe." Jackson doesn't seem happy about that, but I know he won't disobey me. "Mel, keep me updated on the baby, oh and the infant too."

I check the boys, who are sound asleep and head to the packhouse, a central residence for most of the pack members. It has five floors, four above ground and the basement level. In the basement, we have a gym, storerooms and saferooms for the pups and those who can't fight in case of an attack on the Pack. The first floor has the kitchens, main dining hall, a living room of sorts and a game room, which is basically a small arcade, plus a section with just about every gaming console ever made for the pups and teens to use. And some of the adults spent time there, too. Out the back, we have a garden where we grow most of the produce the pack eats. Since the packhouse is practically our community center, we also had a playground built for the pups in the back area. On the other side of the garden, we have another building that is basically a large gym for training which has a basketball court and a few smaller open rooms for small classes. The second floor of the packhouse is where the unmated warriors and omegas who work in the Packhouse live, as well as guest rooms. The third floor is divided into two wings, the Beta wing, where Jackson lives and the Gamma Wing, where John and his mate David live. Our territory has several houses for families around the Packhouse. We also have an apartment building that many families and pack members live in. Then, there's the two schools on the territory, an elementary school and a combination middle school and high school. For a while, we sent the kids from the pack to regular schools, but as we grew, it was easier and safer to build our own schools for the pups. While we did go to the human cities often, many pack members preferred to stay in the territory most of the time to avoid humans, so we had almost everything we needed here.

Riding up the elevator, I wonder if Sara is still awake. It would be nice to get some alone time with her for a change, a rare occurrence with two wild three-year-old boys. Finally reaching my apartment, I find my very pregnant wife asleep on the couch, *How It's Made* playing on the television. So much for my plans for the evening. Turning the television off, I carefully lift my woman and carry her to our bedroom. Laying her on her side on our bed, I adjust her pillows just how she likes them. Chuckling, I slip off her hideous, fuzzy shark slippers. They really are ugly. Brownish, grey fuzz, with fins sticking off the top and sides. A big cartoony smile and embroidered eyes. Just, wow. But she loves them, and I love her. So, the ugly slippers go on the floor on the side of the bed as I tuck her under the blanket for the night, kissing her forehead gently. I know better than to wake a sleeping, pregnant she wolf.

Still chuckling and thinking about the craziness of the past twenty hours, I

grab a quick shower and get in bed with my
beautiful wife to sleep a bit myself.

Chapter Three
Sweet Child O Mine

Beta Jackson

The lights shining down on me are much too bright. Where the hell did I wake up? Reaching out to stretch, my arms can't even move as I am pinned by hard plastic on each side. An incessant beeping fills the room with about a hundred dings a minute.

"How are you feeling this morning, Beta?" a high pitched, way too chipper voice rings in my head over the beeping. I slowly open my eyes and realize I am in the infirmary. Not a fun way to wake up. Pulling the pillow over my face, I roll to my right side, tugging at an IV line in my arm. A small boy, his skin tanned, dark black hair and bandages covering his body sleeps, wires and tubes attached to his tiny form, sleeps in the bed next to mine. Seeing him, all the events of the previous night come back to me. The tiny black wolf, the fight, the little wolf shifting into a little boy, and Melissa. My mate. *Mon petite chére.* I can't smell her. She's not in the room or even nearby.

"Where's Melissa?" I ask, my voice still gruff from sleep. The nurse looked at me, confused.

"Um, who?" the nurse acts like she don't know who I'm talking about. Far as I know, there's only one Melissa in the roughly 100 she wolves in the pack. I look directly at the nurse for the first time. "Miss Melissa, the midwife? She went to the nursery to check on the preemie brought in last night. I can call Doctor Hill for you if you need something, Beta." Her voice is much too seductive, it sickens me. Then, I realize she is one of the many unmated females in the pack who keep trying to seduce me. Definitely not my type. "Miss Melissa only knows about babies and mothers; Doctor Hill can help you better. Unless there's something I can do?"

"Melissa is my mate." Maybe blunt, but the nurse is grossing me out. Even before the mate bond kicked in, she was repulsive to me. She hit on every ranked single male she came across. Ugh. "Can you tell her I'm awake, please." I should just mind-link her, but my head is pounding, and I want to close my eyes again.

"Yes Beta." The nurse's face droops as she turns to leave the room. Damn, I should have asked about the boy's condition. Shielding my eyes from the blazing fluorescent overhead lights with the pillow, I peek out at the boy. *Him looks better* Orion cocks his head and looks out at the boy through my eyes. Our wolves are a separate entity that lives inside us. We work together to control both the human and wolf forms but can see what is going on when the other is in control. Three empty blood bags were stacked on the pole hanging above the infusion machine and a bag of clear fluid with a bright orange label now ran into the IV in his tiny arm.

His chest rises and falls smoothly as he sleeps. The smaller cuts and bruising are gone, thanks to the healing properties of our Lycan genes. Once we have our wolves, we heal faster. Dirt stains the parts of his chest that haven't been cleaned for wound care. His hair is dirty, and he seems very underweight for his size. A white sheet covers him from the waist down.

Using the bed's button, I raise the head of the bed to help me sit up, despite the throbbing remaining in my head. The IV bag attached to my arm is empty, red backing up into the line from my arm. Huh, got that nurse so distracted she didn't check this. This ain't my first infirmary stay, so I know how to disconnect the IV line and leave the plastic bit in my arm. Lowering the side rail between me and the pup, I swing my legs off the bed. The floor here is freezing on my bare feet. Bare and mud covered. Well, got the shorts from last night on still, that's enough. I stand slowly, my pounding head making me dizzy. There's dried blood on my chest and overall, I feel crappy. I'll heal with some more rest and fluids, though, so it is worth it to save this adorable little pup.

I gingerly take a couple steps to the side of the boy's bed. Lowering the rail, I sit on the edge, careful not to squish him or move any of the wires and tubes attached to him. I carefully lift the sheet covering him, noticing he is also covered in mud on his legs and feet. The bandages over the wound on his flank seem freshly changed. I check out the IV bag and see it has Lactated Ringers and doxycycline in it. Ringers is just a fancy name for saline with electrolytes. Doxycycline is an antibiotic. The doc must suspect infection, too.

He starts to stir a little, and then opens his eyes, blinking at the bright lights in the room. Why the nurses insist on leaving the lights on, even when wolves are sleeping, is beyond me.

"Where... Weird sun..." he mumbles, trying to push himself up. Not wanting him to reopen his wounds or hurt himself, I place my hand on his chest gently.

"Don't try to move, Buddy. You're safe, but you're hurt. You don't want to open up your wounds." I try to calm him down. He looks at me, his deep blue eyes wide and dilated and looks around the room.

"Red Wolf?" he asks, looking at me. "You man of Red Wolf? You sniff like dry cow skin. Sparkly lady said find red wolf that sniff of dry cow skin."

"Yeah, Buddy. I'm the red wolf you saw last night. If you mean leather, yeah, I've been told that's what I smell like. My name's Jackson, what's yours?" He still looks scared but relaxes a little when I told him I was the red wolf he saw the night before.

"What a name?" He raises one side of his top lip.

"What do people call you? What do your mom and dad call you?" He looks at me, still confused.

"The Master call-did me 'boy' or 'mutt'. Wadee Sandia call-did me 'brat'. No have mom or dad." He said in a low voice. "The hoomans what give me meat sticks call-did me 'puppy'."

"No one ever gave you a real name?" He tilts his head to the side and wrinkles his little nose. "What's your wolf's name?" I can't believe I am asking a toddler that.

"Him say he 'Thor', but I no have name." I nod at him in understanding.

"Okay. Well, I can't just call you Buddy forever, but we'll stick with that until we figure out a name for you." I pause, thinking about what he said about not having parents. "What happened to your mom and dad?"

"My wolf momma had more pups, so I had to go. No know my people wolf mom." He looks at me, then his eyes got a faraway look. Maybe his wolf was talking to him. "Thor said he can show you people wolf momma."

"How? How can your wolf show me?" The boy sighs and looks like he is unsure of something.

"Need you paw," he reaches out his hand toward me. Intrigued, I put my hand in his. I see Melissa, Leonard and Doc Hill coming in the room as the boy grabs onto my hand and bites me. Hard. The world goes dark.

I feel hands trying to pull my pup off of me. I push the hands away and pull him in closer, mumbling out for whoever it is to stop. Laying on the bed, with the boy tucked close to me, his fangs still in my hand, I find myself suddenly transported to a field. A she wolf lays in the field, giving birth. She looks so familiar.

I approach it slowly, but it doesn't seem to even notice me. She is badly injured, her breathing harsh as she attempts to push out her pup. She looks just like my twin's wolf. Finally, a pitch black wolf pup is born and the female collapses to the ground. She stops breathing, her body shifting to her human form. I am startled to see the humanoid female appear. She wolves rarely give birth in wolf form, most don't even risk shifting during pregnancy because it can harm the pup. Even more startling is when I see who she is. Katrina. She isn't breathing and I can tell she is dead. The pup starts mewing and nudging his nose into Katrina's body. I run over and tried to pick her and the pup up, but my hands just go through them, like they are made of smoke. I watch as a wild wolf came up and carries the newborn pup off. The world goes dark again.

When I open my eyes next, I am back in the Infirmary room, surrounded by my mate, Leonard and Doc Hill. Laying on the boy's bed, holding him close to me. He releases his bite on my hand and goes limp. I look up at Melissa and Leonard. As I catch my breath, I choke out "he's my nephew, he's Katrina's pup."

"What? How can you be sure?" Leonard asks. I tell them what I saw in the boy's memory and what the boy told me before he bit me. "How was he able to show you his memory by biting you? And he was born as a wolf?" as I nod my head at Len, Doc Hill slips the boy out of my arms and starts to recheck his wounds and reattach his wires. *That's my PUP!* Orion growls loud enough for everyone in the room to hear. My jaw drops open. My wolf claimed the boy as his own. It's rare, but our wolf halves can stake a claim on orphaned or endangered pups. The Moon Goddess will recognize the claim and in the case of a ranked shifter, like me, it legitimizes the succession of the rank.

Doc Hill steps away from the boy, raising his hands. Calming my wolf, I attempt to stand from the bed so the Doc can finish working on my son. Lenny reaches to help me stand as Melissa grabs my hand to check the bite. It is already almost healed and barely bled. Melissa wipes the blood off my hand, and it looks like nothing happened.

"That means he's most likely Kade's, too. Those rogues were trying to kill my nephew, too" I can feel Lenny's anger radiating out of him. Kade was the closest Lenny ever had to a real brother. I knew Lenny always felt guilty he couldn't protect Kade better in the battle that took his life. Kade was the son of the Alpha of the neighboring pack. When his parents died in a battle, Lenny's parents took him in, raising the boys as brothers as Lenny's father ran both packs. Kade died in a rogue attack two days before he turned eighteen and the two packs officially merged. So, Len's anger at rogues also being after the boy is no surprise.

Stirring in the bed, the boy pops his eyes open and stares around the room frantically. Looking at Len, he hunches his shoulders down, tilting his head to the side, forcing his tiny body back into the pillow behind him. Leonard's aura must have been affecting him. Lenny is one of the most powerful Alphas in the country, being the son of two Alpha bloodlines. His mother was the daughter of an Alpha, and of course, his father was an Alpha as well. He could make many wolf shifters submit, just by standing near them and letting his aura go. It didn't really affect me much, unless he was angry at me, I'd known him so long. But I didn't want my son scared of my best friend. I look at Leonard imploringly, hoping to give my friend a hint to relax, but not wanting to disrespect my Alpha in front of the doctor or others. Lenny takes a step toward the boy and he cowers down further, wincing and inhaling a sharp breath when he twists his injured sides in the process.

"Dude, Len, please relax a little" I growl softly. Lenny may be my Alpha, but my instincts to protect my pup take over.

"Oh, sorry. I didn't even notice," Len sighs. "I was just... He's Kat's, and maybe Kade's." His shoulders relax as he continues to look at the boy closely. My pup relaxes his neck but still looks at Len with wide eyes. "It's okay, I won't hurt you." Len whispers, reaching out to brush the boy's dark black hair out of his eyes. Turning to me, "he looks just like Kade, except he has Katrina's eyes."

"Hey, Buddy," I brush his scraggly hair out of his face again to look at him, "This is my friend, Alpha Leonard. He won't hurt you, but we're going to need to ask you some questions about what happened to you and who you were running from yesterday, okay?" Both Len and I want to get to the bottom of this quickly and Orion is pestering me to find out why the rogues were chasing him.

"Otay, Red wolf, uh Ja.. Jackson" He looks at me with a tiny smile, then cocks his head to the side like a wolf. "Do you know my people wolf momma?"

"Yeah, Bud, I do. Well, did..." I pause. "Your wolf shifter momma was my sister, Bud. You're my nephew and I'm going to take care of you now. You're gonna live with me, and hopefully my mate, Melissa. Okay?" I point to Melissa and give her a little grin when I mention her. Len nods at me, silently giving me the okay to say that. Technically, I should have asked him for permission before I basically told the boy he could live in our pack, but I was certain Len was going to be okay with it. The boy is his nephew, too. The boy nods once, raising the sides of his lips and wrinkling his nose

Alpha Leonard

Jackson told us the boy didn't have a name, but his wolf's name is Thor. Since we know he is Katrina's child, there's a good chance he is also Kade's. Jax said in the memory Thor showed him, the boy was born while Katrina was in her wolf form, as a wolf. I just need to figure out how he survived and what happened to him in the three years since Katrina was found dead. We knew Katrina was murdered by rogues in the middle of July three years ago. Her body was found by her mate's pack members in the woods of the human territory in Marin and taken to the Berkeley Pack for autopsy. At the time, Doctor Hill was at the Berkeley Pack and was the one to perform the autopsy. His report didn't mention her giving birth or even signs of pregnancy though.

"Doctor Hill," I turn to the doc, "Did you find any evidence of pregnancy when you did the autopsy on Katrina?"

"No, Alpha," he replies, looking at Jackson with some trepidation, "but if she was in wolf form when she gave birth and shifted right after, it may have erased any evidence. I had no history on her when she was brought in. It wasn't even until I was done with the autopsy that I found out she was mated to our Beta."

"Hmm." I stall for time, not knowing how to proceed at this point. The boy can't be more than three, so he probably won't be the best storyteller. And who knows how much he remembers. I can't rely on him just biting Jackson again to get more details. "Okay, little guy. We really need to figure out a name for you, but how about I call you Buddy, too?" The boy nods slowly. "Can you tell me how you got hurt, Buddy?"

"Um," the boy looks over to Jackson, who nods in encouragement. "The bad people wolves hurt me because the Master said I was bad. But I'm not a bad pup. I be a good pup."

"People wolves?"

"It's what he calls wolf shifters. I don't think he has ever been specifically told much about us." Jackson replies.

"Yeah, wolves that can be peoples, like hoomans, but wolves." The boy tries to explain. It was like trying to have a conversation with my boys, but this little guy clearly doesn't know much about our kind. He called the shifter that had him hurt "The Master", though. I wonder if he is talking about the same evil rogue leader Jackson and I were fighting against for years. It is likely with the wolfsbane that was in his injuries.

"Can you tell me more about this 'Master' you mentioned?" The boy's eyes start watering, his little body shaking.

"It's okay, Buddy," Jax rubs on the boy's shoulder, "No one will hurt you again; I'll make sure of it."

"Ohh.. O tay..." the boy whimpers. "He a mean people wolf... I mean shipper."

"Shifter, Buddy, not ship." Jax gently corrects him. "Shift."

"Uh. Shift er.." the little guy starts again. "He mean. He take all sorts of wolves and peoples and make them do bad things or do bad things to them. He try make me make other pups dead. I no want make any pup dead." He stops and looks at Jax, with worry in his eyes. "I need get bank-it from twee. Has little pup. I no want little pup to dead." He sits up, trying to disentangle himself from the wires. Jax stops him gently before he can hurt himself.

"It's okay, Buddy. We have her. I'm helping her get stronger here in another room. Can you tell us anything about her?" Melissa softly asks the boy.

"Pup momma help me 'scape from Master. The bad wolves deaded her as we was running way from camp. I ran wiff pup. Master wanted to dead pup because pup girl and Wadee Sandia 'sper ment' no work. Master no want girl pups. He make girl pups dead, but all pups be girls, so he make them all dead. Wadee Sandia only keep pups that she tink have powers. Makes bad wolves dead them. Master try make me dead the little pups, but I will not." Rage fills every adult in the room as the boy tells us about this "Master". He must be talking about the same evil rogue we had been fighting. There can't be two wolves out there that evil, can there? The Sandia person, though, I have no idea who that is.

"Pup momma no wanted little pup to dead, and she say she knew my peep... shifter momma. Say she want help me. She say, I run this way and find other people wolves who can help us. And din, I find Red Wolf who smell like dry cow skin, like sparkly lady said to find when I sleep." His voice raises an octave when he says the last part. "But, Master, he try to make me dead, too. He say since I no use my special powers for him and I no teach his boy pup how to be wolf, I no good to him."

"What special powers?" Jackson asks, raising one side of his lip and tilting his head, a slight snarl underscoring his confusion. He is clearly mad at the Master's actions, but I think the boy does not understand that.

"I... uh... um.. Peas don't be mad. I try be good and no use power." Tears well up in his eyes as he looks at Jackson.

Beta Jackson

Shit, I scared him. "I'm not mad at you, Bud", I gently pull him into a hug as I try to reassure him, while trying not to disturb his wounds. "I'm just angry that the Master hurt you and tried to take you away from me before I even got to see you." I rub his little head, messing up his hair before gently nuzzling his forehead with mine, a common form of affection between wolves and shifters alike. "Nobody's ever going to hurt my boy again, I promise." I whisper softly into his ear, even though I know all the wolves in the room can hear me anyway. He smiles slightly as one tear escapes his eye and he sniffles.

"So, Buddy, what do you mean by special powers?" I ask a bit more gently than the first time.

"I can make owies go away," he replies.

"You can heal yourself? Most shifters can do that..." Doctor Hill raised one eyebrow at my boy as my boy glares at him with the most adorable scowl ever.

"No! I make udder wolf people's owies go away, too. And manimals and hoomans' owies." The little guy glares at the doc and sticks his tongue out seemingly annoyed that the doctor didn't understand him. He is so cute when he is frustrated. "And I can make people hurt like fire touched dem. By just touching dem, I put fire in dem. I can make fire in weaves and sticks, too" He adds, glaring at the doctor as if waiting for the doctor to say that was normal for shifter, too.

"Whoa," Leonard's jaw drops. Hell, I am shocked, too. It's rare for wolf shifters to have any special powers, but clearly this little guy is no average shifter. He was born able to shift and could heal and hurt others by touch. "Kade used to say he had the ability to burn people by just touching them. He said it was some power passed down in his family from a dragon shifter ancestor. I never believed him, until I saw him burn a rogue one day. I still don't believe the dragon story, though. I've never heard of a shifter that could heal other creatures, though."

"Do you think Elder Kyah would know more?" my beautiful mate speaks up. Orion wants to mark and mate her right here, and is making it obvious, my shorts getting tighter the longer we look at her. *She is so pretty,* Orion murmurs in my head while jumping around in circles. I take a deep breath to calm him with her scent.

"I'll talk to him," Lenny replies. "Jax, I know it's been a rough night, but I do need your report of the attack as soon as possible. I want to go to the Council with what we have learned."

"Yes, Alpha. But should we tell the Council about the boy? I am worried they may try to take him and 'study' him," which for the Council meant they would experiment on him. He doesn't need any more of that crap in his life.

"I'm going to mention him, but none of his powers or even his connection to Katrina and Kade. I think we need to keep as much as possible about him a secret. I don't trust everyone on the Council, nor do I think we are rid of the Master." Leonard's voice deepens to his Alpha command voice before he speaks the next part "No one outside this room is to know about him. We will tell the pack that you rescued an orphaned rogue and have chosen to adopt him. Understood?" Everyone except my boy nods their understanding. The little guy looks at me with his head cocked.

"What's 'dopt?"

I explained what adoption is to the little guy and he seemed excited. He said he was looking forward to having a real family of his own. The nurse brought in some lunch for both him and me. He didn't know how to eat with utensils, so I planned to teach him once I got him out of this infirmary. Infirmary patients, unless on a medically prescribed diet, were served the same food that the Omegas made for the Packhouse lunch, so it wasn't bad. We had ravioli with meatballs and French bread. My little guy made a huge mess trying to eat ravioli with his hands. He got all the pasta and meatballs in him, but the sauce went *everywhere*. I think he managed to get more covered in the red sauce than he was in blood last night. I cleaned him up with a washcloth from the bathroom, but the nurse had to change his bandages because they were covered in sauce, too. I peeked at the wounds, and they were almost healed but still visible. He was going to have scars, but he was going to get better. After he ate, he was tired, so I held him while the nurse changed his sheets. He fell asleep in my arms and I gently laid him in the now clean bed so he could nap.

I now sit in a chair next to him, working on my reports for Leonard on my laptop. I'd had one of the warriors bring it to me from my office. Music plays softly through the speakers, trying to drown out the noises of the infirmary so I can concentrate, but not so loud it will wake my pup. I hate doing paperwork and the slightest noises can distract me easily. I get a notification of a new email from Lenny. Paperwork I need to fill out to do the adoption for the little guy. I realize I need to sit down with Melissa to go over this. Accepting me as her mate means accepting him as well. So much happened in the last 24 hours, it was life changing for more than just me and the boy.

The implications of the events of the past twenty-four hours are mind boggling. Everything in my life is changing. I am the Beta of the largest pack in Northern California. I've become the father of a three-year-old overnight. I found my mate, who I still haven't even sat down with to discuss our new life together. That is if she wants a life with me, she keeps telling me she needs to talk first. This is a lot.

My boy starts to wake up from his nap. His little head nods and his little fingers tap out the drum beats of the song playing. Metallica's *For Whom the Bell Tolls*, one of the harder songs to play drums on.

"I like these sounds. The hoomans dat wear dry cow skin and ride horses wif wheels wisten to this. At the human cave. I like dem. Dey toss me meat sticks and big chunks of meat." Well, well... My boy likes Metallica. "I specially like the part that go..." He holds his little hands up and moved them up and down fast, almost like he is drumming and shakes his head back and forth. It is so cute. Here I am, a big tough guy, and all I can think about is how adorable this boy is and how gorgeous my mate is.

"This song? This is Metallica. They are the greatest metal band in the world." I smile at him. "The beats are made on drums. I'll show you my drum set when you move in with me after the doctor gets you out of here, okay?" He smiles at me, happier than I'd seen him since I met him.

"I like the dums. Dey remind me of paw beats on the ground." Still tapping his fingers in rhythm with the drums, he is getting into the music as it switches to another Metallica song. Amazingly, he is keeping up with the beat precisely, as if he is Lars Ulrich himself.

"Hey, maybe that's a good name for you..." He cocks his head at me. "Lars. The drummer, the guy who makes those beats for Metallica, is named Lars Ulrich. It's a Danish and German name, so it would match well with 'Thor', too, since he was a god in the old Nordic culture." He looks at me, confused, but thinking. I see his eyes go hazy, like he is talking to his wolf.

"I no know what lot of dos words mean, but Thor and me like it. I want be call-did Lars." He smiles at me.

"Okay, Lars Broussard. I think it sounds pretty good."

"Bro-sad?" He tries to repeat my, well our, last name quizzically.

"Brew-sard, I clarified for him. It's our surname. The name that means we are a family. Lars is you, what people will call you. Broussard is your, and my, last name, what most members of our family share. It means 'man of the forest' in Cajun French. My great, great, great grandparents came to this country from France, through what's now called Canada. We're part Cajun." He raises his eyebrows, confused again. I chuckle at him "Don't worry, Lars, I'll explain it more over time." He smiles back at first, then his eyebrows scrunch up again.

"You my Pa now. Do I have a new ma now, too?" Wow, how do I answer this one? I'm not even sure if he does. Would

Melissa want to be his mom? Did she even want me? We hadn't really talked much with how chaotic the past day had been.

"I don't know yet, Buddy. I am still figuring that out myself." It was all I could honestly tell him at this point.

Chapter Four
Mother

Lady Melissa

Being the only midwife on the medical staff, I'm back at work with no sleep. My body aches with exhaustion, but my heart feels light as I check on the tiny she-pup the boy rescued. She's a fighter—her breathing is strong and steady, even without extra oxygen, a miracle considering her underdeveloped lungs. She eagerly drinks formula and is steadily gaining weight, her resilience shining through. For a preemie, she's thriving against the odds. Part of me wants to take her home myself, but I know I need to talk to Jackson first.

Jackson. My pulse quickens just thinking about him. He's already preparing to raise his nephew, the boy who saved her. There's so much we need to discuss about us, about our future. Most importantly, I need to tell him my truth: I can't have children. It's a cruel twist of fate for many shifters, especially Betas and Alphas, where legacy means everything. My first fated mate rejected me when he learned the truth, blaming the scars left by a rogue attack in my teens. The rejection nearly broke me. I can't survive another.

Melissa?

A deep, familiar Cajun accent fills my mind through the pack's mental link. My wolf, Artemis, springs to life, her excitement almost overwhelming. *It's mate!*

Jackson? I respond, even though I already know. Of course, it's Jackson.

Yeah... um, can we talk? Like, in person? He hesitates. *I'm still with Lars. Can you come to his room when you get a chance?*

Lars? I blink, confused. I don't recall anyone in the pack by that name. The only Lars I know is the drummer from Metallica. As much as I'd love to meet him, I doubt a rock star is hanging out in an infirmary on shifter territory.

Jackson chuckles through the link. *The little guy and I picked a name. He likes drumbeats, especially heavy metal, so we went with Lars. He approves.*

That's a great name, I reply, smiling. I glance down at the tiny she-pup, giving her a gentle nuzzle before ensuring she's warm and settled. After updating my assistant, I make my way to Lars' room.

When I reach the doorway, my breath catches. Jackson sits beside the boy, explaining different metal bands with the enthusiasm of a superfan. Snippets of music play from his phone as Lars nods along, tapping his fingers on the tray in rhythm. Despite everything he's endured, the boy looks... content.

Jackson glances up and sees me, his face lighting up with a smile that sends chills racing through me. "Hey, Lars, buddy, I'm going to step out for a bit, okay? You keep listening, and I'll be back soon." Lars nods, his small face solemn but understanding.

Jackson meets me at the door, pulling me into a hug. His voice drops to a whisper. "Hello, *mon chére.*" His breath brushes against my ear, sending shivers down my spine. "Let's take a walk."

We step into the hall, his large hand engulfing mine. My heart pounds. I have to tell him. Now. Before I lose my nerve.

"I need to tell you something, Jackson," I begin, my voice trembling.

He stops, turning to face me. "*Mon chére*, you're my mate, a gift from the Moon Goddess herself. Nothing—"

I press my fingers gently against his lips, silencing him. The sparks of our bond flare at the touch, but I force myself to focus. "Don't say something you might not be able to live up to. Just let me explain first." He nods, his brow furrowing, but his gaze remains steady.

"When I was fourteen, a rogue attack almost killed me," I say, the memory a sharp blade in my chest. "One of them slashed my abdomen, and I nearly bled out. The doctor saved my life, but not my uterus. I can't have pups, Jackson."

His eyes darken, and a low growl rumbles in his chest. I know he remembers that attack: it's the same one that took his parents. "I found my first mate when I turned eighteen," I continue, swallowing the lump in my throat. "He rejected me the moment I told him. He said a Beta couldn't have a barren mate." My voice cracks, and a tear escapes. Jackson's thumb brushes it away.

"*Mon chére*, that Beta was a fool. And more so for being a Dodgers fan." His attempt at humor coaxes a small laugh from me. "I'll never leave you because of an injury or anything else. I don't need pups to love you. I don't need heirs. I just need *you*." He cups my face, his rough thumb tracing my cheek. "You're my mate. My forever. I already have a pup now, or will as soon as I finish this mountain of paperwork to adopt Lars."

Tears blur my vision as his words sink in. Before I can speak, Jackson pulls me close, his lips brushing against my forehead, then my cheeks, and finally the sensitive spot on my neck where he would one day mark me.

"I want forever with you," he murmurs.

"Jackson, I..." I can't finish. My heart is too full. He smiles, his thumb grazing my lip.

"Let's check on the little girl. She needs us too, doesn't she?"

I nod, slipping my hand into his. Together, we head down the hall, ready to face whatever comes next—together.

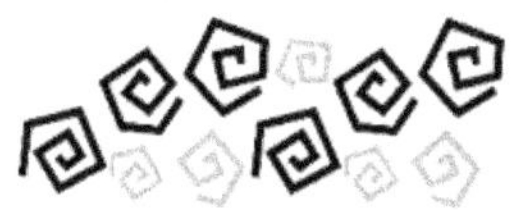

Beta Jackson

I can't believe it. Melissa wants to raise Lars with me. Relief floods through me, washing away the anxiety I hadn't even realized had taken root. I was so worried. She-wolves often lean into their "survival of the fittest" instincts when it comes to pups, especially ones they aren't blood-related to. It's a trait tied to our animalistic nature, but I know Melissa is different. She's always been different. Her willingness to take Lars in solidifies it for me—she's the mate I've always dreamed of, and maybe, just maybe, we can build a family together.

As we head down the hall to check on the baby girl Lars had been protecting, I hold Melissa's hand, feeling the warmth of her touch spread through me. It's grounding, yet electrifying, and for a moment, everything feels like it's falling into place.

But then, just as we reach the nursery, a voice breaks through my mind-link, shattering my calm. *Beta, uh… we have a problem.* It's one of the nurses from Lars's room. Her tone is hesitant, nervous.

What happened? I demand, dread curling in my stomach.

The boy is missing. I went to check on him, and… I can't find him anywhere.

WHAT?! The roar tears through me before I can stop it, panic tightening its grip. *How does a toddler hooked up to IVs just disappear? The windows don't even open!*

Out loud, I manage to say, "*Mon chére*, Lars is missing. I have to get back to his room." My voice shakes with the effort to stay calm, but inside, I'm spiraling. It hasn't even been twenty-four hours, and I've already lost my pup? What kind of father loses his kid in a hospital?

Melissa places a hand on my arm, her touch steadying me. "Jackson, calm down. He's not missing… although I have no idea how he got past us without us seeing him." She points toward the crib in the nursery.

I follow her gaze and freeze. There, standing next to the crib in his untied hospital gown—bare toddler butt on full display—is Lars. He's staring at the tiny infant girl, his small hand gently rubbing hers.

He looks up at us, his white teeth flashing in a hopeful grin. "We keep her? She need ma and pa, too. We make her a Bro-sad, too?" His big, pleading eyes lock onto mine, and I know in that moment I'm doomed. There's no way I'll ever be able to say no to this kid.

I glance at Melissa, trying to gauge her reaction. She steps forward, her expression soft. "Lars, we'll have to see, okay? There are rules we need to follow. Since she's an orphan, we have to check if she has any other family. But until then, we can take care of her. Does that sound good?"

He toddles over to her, his IV bag clutched in one hand, and hugs her tightly. His unsteady steps make it clear he's still in pain, but the determination in his tiny face is unwavering.

"Lars, how did you get here from your room?" I ask, crouching to his level.

"I climb-did down from the big nest and walked here. I hear wittle pup crying. I follow cries. No want wittle pup cry, ever. I 'tect wittle pup. Tolded her momma I willed." His little voice is so serious it almost breaks me.

"And the IV pole?" I press.

"Metal stick falled over, so I brought dis wiff me. Took off sappy circles from my belly, doh."
I sigh, tying his gown to cover his bare bottom.

"And what happened to the diaper the nurses put on you?"

"Diaper gross. Left in room wiff ucky water bowl. Someone peed in water bowl: it sniff bad." He wrinkles his nose in disgust. "I pee on twees and rocks. No need weird butt cover dat stink like pee. Make hungry maminals find me." He pauses, shaking his head as if clearing a thought. "And I make my sniff small when I go by you. Pups no 'posta 'sturb big wolves talking."

"What do you mean, make your scent small?" I ask, frowning. Another rare power?

"I need not be sniffed, so I make sniff not big." He shrugs like it's obvious, leaving me with more questions than answers.

Before I can probe further, Lars's eyes droop. "Widdle pup sleep now. Me sleepy, too."

His exhaustion is evident, and I don't hesitate to scoop him up. He rests his head on my shoulder, his tiny body relaxing against mine as his breathing evens out.

Melissa watches us from beside the crib, her fingers gently rubbing the baby girl's belly. "What do you think about all this?" I ask, my voice soft.

Before she can answer, a small sound interrupts us, a rumble from the infant's tiny butt.

"Did she just... fart?" I ask, staring at the baby in disbelief.

"Yup," Melissa replies, laughing—a sound so beautiful it makes my chest ache. "Girls fart too, Beta."

Her teasing smile lights up her face, and I can't resist leaning in to kiss her. As her lips meet mine, everything feels right.

"Lars is special," she whispers against my lips. "This momma will definitely have her hands full with these two." She points to herself with a grin before pulling back to gently kiss my cheek.

I hold Lars tighter, glancing at the tiny girl in the crib. Somehow, I know this chaotic, mismatched family is exactly what I've been waiting for.

Chapter Five

We're a Happy Family

Alpha Leonard

The sound of Alex and Tony giggling carries from the playroom attached to my office. They're laughing at something Bear said to Ojo on *Bear in the Big Blue House*, their current favorite show. Normally, Sara wouldn't allow screen time this early in the day, but with both boys stuck in casts, she made an exception. She's off working on new schedules for the teens on summer break with Gamma John's mate, David.

I sit at my desk, awaiting Jackson, Melissa, Doctor Hill, and Elder Kyah for a meeting about the rescued children. Doctor Hill discharged all three boys this morning, but Melissa insisted the baby girl remain in the NICU under observation until a permanent home is established for her.

From the look in Jackson's eyes yesterday, I suspect he intends for that home to be his.

Footsteps echo down the hall. A knock sounds at my door, and Jackson enters with the little boy perched on one arm and Melissa's hand in his. Elder Kyah and Doctor Hill follow closely behind. As Jackson walks past the playroom, I nod toward the door, and he gets the hint, pulling it shut.

Before it closes, the boy catches a glimpse of the TV and freezes, eyes wide. "What's that?" he whispers, his small finger pointing in awe. I'd almost forgotten—he's spent most of his life in the wild. Has he ever even seen a television? Sara would be thrilled if our boys were that sheltered.

Jackson smiles and explains gently. "That's a television. After we talk to Alpha Leonard, maybe you can watch a show with his boys. Okay?"

The boy's head tilts as he considers this. "Udder pups live here?" he asks, his tiny voice tinged with worry. "Are dey mean pups?"

"Lots of pups live here," Jackson assures him, nuzzling the boy's forehead as he lowers him onto his lap. "And no, they're not mean. I think you'll be good friends with them."

Satisfied for the moment, the boy relaxes against Jackson, clutching his shirt. Melissa sits beside them, and Jackson pulls her close. His sheer size makes the couch a more logical choice than the stiff wooden chairs by my massive redwood desk. Elder Kyah and Doctor Hill settle into the chairs, their expressions somber but focused.

I lean forward, addressing the boy. "So, buddy, I need to ask you some questions about yourself and what happened before you came here. Is that okay?"

The boy nods, offering a small smile. "Okay, Alpha. I Lars Bro-sad now. Lars will help." His innocent pride tugs at my heart, even as I glance at Jackson in disbelief. Of course, Jackson would name the kid after a heavy metal musician. When we were kids, his pets included dogs named Ozzy and Motley and a turtle named Lemmy. Jackson catches my look and shrugs, smirking.

"What? It fits."

Shaking my head, I turn back to Lars. "All right, Lars. Yesterday, you told us about someone you called 'The Master.' Can you tell us more about him and his group? We think he's a very bad man, and we want to stop him from hurting anyone else."

Lars' tiny face grows serious, his gaze flicking up to Jackson as though seeking permission. Jackson nods gently, and Lars begins.

"The Master, he bad, bad man," Lars starts, his voice quiet but resolute. "After my wolf momma had more pups, I had to go live with my brudders as a wolf. But I not real wolf like dem, so I stay Thor. Thor is me. I go where hoomans live, but dey not shift like me either. Dey call me 'pupper' and throw meat sticks. Dey drink burny water and ride metal horses wif wheels."

I glance at Jackson, who seems as bewildered as I am, but neither of us interrupts. Lars takes a deep breath and continues, his small hands gripping the edge of Jackson's shirt.

"One day, I saw people-wolf in da woods. Him fight wif a she-hooman, but she not hooman. She witch. I not know den, but later, I hear she called Lady Sandia. Dey talk about a plan. Later, I find out da plan was me."

The room grows still as Lars recounts how the witch and the Master's group captured him, experimented on him, and used his powers to harm others. His innocent words paint a horrifying picture: female pups murdered at birth, soldiers brutalizing captive women, and children forced into combat.

As Lars speaks, I notice Jackson's hands tighten protectively around him, his knuckles white. When Lars describes the beatings he endured at the hands of the Master's son, Arioch, Jackson's face flushes with anger. Melissa reaches over, placing a calming hand on his arm.

Lars' voice wavers as he recalls the escape. "The widdle pup's momma, she give her to me. Say I take her to safe place, here. I run so fast. I hear bad wolves catch her, but I keep runnin'. I hide widdle pup in tree. Bad wolves find me, but I claw back. I make fire. Then I see Red Wolf. Him smell like dried cow skin. Moon sparkly lady say find Red Wolf and I safe. She was right."

When he finishes, Jackson pulls him close, resting his forehead against the boy's. "That's right. You're safe now, Lars," he whispers.

I clear my throat, glancing toward the playroom door, where the sound of Alex and Tony giggling continues. "Hey, Lars," I say, trying to lighten the mood, "how about you go watch a cartoon with Alex and Tony while we talk a little more? They'd love to meet you."

Jackson stands, carrying Lars to the playroom. "All right, boys, this is Lars. Be nice, and no jumping on him," he warns. The boys' enthusiastic greetings make Lars stiffen at first, but Jackson reassures him, and soon the three are watching TV together.

Returning to my desk, I fix Jackson with a look. "Clearly, you plan to take custody of Lars. Did you finish the paperwork?"

Jackson hesitates, his cheeks pink. "Not yet. I wasn't sure what to put in the

'Mother' section. Things have been... busy."

Melissa smiles, taking his hand. "Put my name down, Jax. He's ours."

Jackson blinks at her, stunned, before grinning. "Forever?"

"Forever," she replies softly.
"Well, that's settled," I say, chuckling. "Now, about the girl. If we declare her an orphan, she can be adopted."

"We'll take her," Melissa and Jackson say in unison.
The room falls quiet for a moment before Elder Kyah bursts out laughing. "You're really going all in, huh, Jax? Have you thought about names?"
"Janis," Jackson says instantly.
"Nope," I say flatly. "We're not naming her after Janis Joplin. How about Elizabeth? Melissa's mother's name."

Jackson smirks. "Perfect. But I'm calling her Lizzy, after Halestorm's lead singer." Melissa rolls her eyes, but her smile says she wouldn't have it any other way.

Chapter Six
Beautiful With You

Lady Melissa

Alpha Leonard kindly offered to watch Lars with his boys, giving Jackson and me a rare moment alone. We haven't had much of a chance since we met, what with the chaos of getting Lars and Elizabeth settled and Elizabeth still in the NICU. It's been less than 48 hours since we first crossed paths, but for shifters, that's a lifetime to go without marking one's mate. And mating.

Here we are now, in Jackson's apartment—the logical place for us to start our family. The Beta Apartment is designed for family life, with more than enough rooms for the kids to each have their own space. It's huge. Right now, it feels more like a guest room than a home. I've been living in a single room, so the sheer size is overwhelming. We need to furnish it for the kids, but Jackson already has a king-size bed in our room, which is a start.

He shows me around, leading me into the ensuite bathroom and the walk-in closet. I can't help but notice it's eerily empty for a man who should have more clothes than a few random items strewn about. He's a Beta, after all—he should have suits, regular clothes, something that shows off his status.

"Where are all your clothes?" I ask, raising an eyebrow. Jackson casually points to a dresser in the main bedroom, then at a chair where a black suit jacket and pants are carelessly tossed over. I blink, realizing I've never seen him wear anything but shorts, T-shirts, and slides since I met him.

"Is that your only suit?" I can't help but ask, trying to suppress a laugh.

Jackson saunters over to the dresser and pulls out a pair of swim trunks. "Got a bathing suit," he smirks. "And a birthday suit." His words are smooth, playful, and laced with something deeper, a hint of intent. He moves toward me, predatory in his approach. "I don't want to talk about clothes, Mon chére. We'll get yours here later, and I'm fine with what I have. Alpha knows I hate suits. He rarely makes me wear them."

Before I can say anything else, he pulls his T-shirt off, tossing it carelessly into the laundry bin. He steps toward me, his hands settling on my hips as he gently pulls me closer. His gaze locks on mine, and there's an intensity there, something primal. "I am going to kiss you. Then, I would love nothing more than to finally claim you—completely. Mine." His words are low, full of promise, and before I can even catch my breath, his lips meet mine.

His kiss is slow at first, coaxing a response from me, but it deepens, his hands moving up from my hips to cradle my head. A shiver runs through me as I feel every inch of him. Every touch, every breath, is building something impossible to resist.
I can't ignore the doubts creeping in, though. He's assured me more times than I can count that my infertility doesn't matter—that our children, Lars and Elizabeth, are proof enough of our bond. But I still feel like I'm not enough. Not for

him. Not for someone who looks like a Greek God and is everything I'm not.

I'm short for a shifter, barely five foot five. My hair's plain, brown, and usually tossed into a messy braid. The only thing that makes me stand out are my hazel eyes, a mixture of brown and green. Jackson? He's six foot six, solid muscle, with a six-pack I'd happily spend hours licking. His red hair... it's wild, and I can't stop thinking about how much I want to tie him to a bed, or have him tie me up. How could someone like him want someone as average as me?

Suddenly, Jackson pulls back, his thumb gently tilting my chin up so he can look into my eyes. "Mon chére, what's wrong?" he asks, his voice full of concern. I realize I've stopped kissing him, my insecurities flooding in like a tide.

"Are you really sure about me?" My voice cracks as the question slips out, a raw fear I can't hide. The weight of rejection feels like a phantom pressing down on me, and I don't know if I can bear it again. A single tear escapes before I can stop it.

Before I can even register what's happening, Jackson sweeps me off my feet, kissing the tear away as he carries me to the bed. He lays me gently down, his voice a low growl in my ear. "My beautiful mate," he murmurs. "You are perfect. Gorgeous." He brushes a lock of hair from my face, his touch sending a thrill through me. "If you can't hear my words telling you how much I love you, let me show you. Let me show you how much your body turns me on."

He takes my hand and guides it to the hard bulge pressing against his shorts. His words, his touch, make me dizzy, and he doesn't stop there. "I'm going to worship your body until you have no doubt how certain I am that I want to be with you. Then, I'll claim you—mark you—so the entire world knows you're mine and mine alone."

Jackson kisses me again, more deeply this time, his hands roaming, his touch sparking fire across my skin. He slides his hand up my dress, his fingers brushing against the edge of my panties. Every touch feels like electricity coursing through me, igniting a fire I can't ignore. He moves with purpose, one finger tracing delicate circles, sending shockwaves of pleasure through me. His kiss is relentless, his tongue teasing, demanding.

His scent—leather and rum—surrounds me, intoxicating. It's heady, addictive. And then, his voice whispers against my lips: "Cum for me, Mon chére."

The words break through the haze of desire, and I shatter. Waves of pleasure crash over me, leaving me gasping, my body trembling as I release. I feel myself drenching his hand as I ride the high, my heart pounding. As I begin to come back down, Jackson pulls me even closer, his arm around me, grounding me in the aftershocks.

"My beautiful mate," he murmurs, his hand stroking my back, making me shiver in his embrace. "You're perfect, just as you are." He kisses my forehead, his hand sliding down my spine, undoing my bra clasp with a deft motion. "Can I take these off?" His voice is rough, laden with need. He tugs at my panties, and I nod, unable to speak as I'm overwhelmed with emotion.

Jackson's hands work with a purpose, taking my dress off, my body fully exposed. I reach down, unbuttoning his shorts, my fingers trembling with anticipation. When they finally slide down, I freeze—staring at him, my mouth hanging open.

"Mon chére, alright?" He lifts my chin gently, his gaze tender as I realize I've been staring at him in awe. My face burns with embarrassment.

"You're huge," I mutter, barely audible, hoping my words are too jumbled to understand. Jackson smirks, clearly amused by my reaction. But then he leans in, kissing me again, deep and slow. He pulls back, resting his forehead against mine. "Beautiful, you were made for me." He kisses my cheek. "I'll fit, and I'll make you fly again."

His hands lift my dress over my head, taking my bra with it. "But first," he says, his voice full of desire, "I need to taste every inch of you."

Beta Jackson

Kissing down Melissa's neck, there's one spot that makes her moan more than the rest. I graze my canines along the spot where her neck meets her shoulder. Reaching down to cup her mound, I rub my finger on her clit as I gently nip at the spot where I will mark her soon. How did a rough Cajun boy like me get so lucky to be mated to such a gorgeous woman? She pushes her chest into me as I increase the pressure on her clit slightly. Her perfect breasts are begging to be licked, so I drag myself away from her neck to begin kissing and licking them. I promised her I was going to taste every inch of hers, and I don't break my promises.

Slipping one finger into her pussy, I curve it up to a slightly rougher area of flesh inside her, drawing moans from her that are making my already stiff dick impossibly harder. Fuck, I might explode just from listening to her reactions to me worshiping her. Pumping my finger in and out of her, I coax more and more of her beautiful moans out until she tenses up, screams out my name and coats my hand with her juices. Grinning at her, I lick the juices off my fingers before claiming her mouth once again.

"Jackson," we break our kiss to breathe, Melissa moaning out my name in her post orgasm haze. "Jackson, I need you." Thrusting her hips towards me, her mound grazes my hard cock, making me twitch. The sparks of the mate bond roll through my body as she rubs herself on my rod. Groaning, I roll us so she lays on her back, positioning myself between her legs, holding my body up on one arm to avoid crushing her. My other hand holds the back of her head, controlling our kiss. Positioning my tip at her entrance, I break our kiss to look into her eyes.

"Are you ready, *Mon chére?*" Goddess, I hope I don't hurt her. Despite my reassurance to her, our size difference is a concern of mine. She nods, her gaze intense as she stares softly into my eyes. I see the flicker of desire in them. In this moment, nothing else exists, just her and I. Her scent surrounds me, laced with the strong scent of her desire. Slowly, I slide myself into her. Her body tenses at the intrusion. Damn she's so tight, I'm not sure I'll fit any further.

"Relax, beautiful," kissing along her jaw and down her neck, I run my hand along her shoulder and arm, sparks tingling everywhere our bodies connect. "Breathe. Breathe in my scent, my love." She takes a deep breath, her body melting into my arm as relaxation overtakes her. As the tension leaves her, my cock slides into her, seating me deep in her tight pussy. Her walls squeeze my cock, sending sparks straight to my core. Holding my lower half as still as I can as she stretches to accommodate my girth, I plant kisses on every inch of exposed skin I can reach. "Breathe Baby. I've got you, *Mon chére.*"

After what feels like an eternity of being seated inside her, sparks shooting through my core, Melissa wraps her legs around my hips, whispering in my ear, begging me to move. Staring into her eyes, cautious of any sign of pain, I pull out slowly and just as slowly sink back into her. Her moans of pleasure encourage me. Pumping in and out of her tightness, I gradually increase the speed of my thrusts, in and out, deep and shallow, varying the thrust as her pleasure rises once more. I know I won't be able to hold out in her perfect pussy much longer. As she gets closer and closer to the cliff, I reach down to her hard nub, my mouth kissing and sucking the sensitive spot on her neck, preparing it for my mark. Rubbing small, firm circles on her nub, pumping in and out at a frenzied pace, she breathes out my name as she falls over the edge. Sinking my fangs into the spot on her neck, I explode inside her, marking her inside and out as mine.

"Mine," Orion growling along with me around our fangs in her neck. Melissa goes limp, her eyes closing beneath me as her body forces her to sleep as the mark takes. I retract my fangs, sliding my cock out of her. Rolling us to our sides, I gather her close to me, wrapping my body around hers, protectively. Kissing her forehead,

"Sleep, *mon petite chere*, sleep." I whisper as I close my eyes as well to rest.

Chapter Seven
Dr. Feelgood

Alex and Tony are propped up on the cozy couch, eyes wide with excitement at the moving pictures on the glass screen surrounded by a black box in front of them. Lars approaches with a puzzled look after Jackson left to go back to the meeting with the Alpha.

"Hey," Lars nervously greets the boys, apprehension apparent in his eyes. His only experiences before with other shifter pups have been bad, either the mean Arioch at the Master's camp, or the injured little pups in Sandia's lab. "What is that?" Lars points at the moving pictures on the screen.

Tony, the outgoing one, grins. "It's Bear in the Big Blue House. It's our favorite tv show."

Still confused, "What's tv?" Lars raises an eyebrow, looking between the two boys.

Incredulous, Alex's jaw drops, "You've never heard of tv?" He points at the black box on the wall. "That's a tv." He says blankly.

"Does it only show the Bear show?" Lars tilts his head to the side, watching the weird orange furry creature. It doesn't look like any bears Lars has ever seen.

Tony shakes his head, "no, silly." He begins to chuckle. "It has all sorts of stuff. Mickey Mouse, animal shows, Daddy even watches a show about two brothers who hunt silly versions of other supernatural creatures. Momma says the tall brother is cute."

Alex nods enthusiastically. "Yeah! It's like a magic box that shows you all kinds of stuff!"

Lars is intrigued, tilting his head to the other side wolfishly. "So, it's like the pictures on cave walls. It tells stories, but they move?" Alex and Tony exchanged puzzle glances before tilting their own heads, jaws dropped. "Kind of! It's like exploring, but with pictures that move!"

Lars sits down to watch the tv with them. The three become fast friends, chatting and giggling at the orange furry creature on the television that Alex says is named Bear. Bear is a friendly pretend bear. Lars tells the other boys that real bears aren't very friendly, and he's pretty sure they don't sing. The boys sit, talk and blend their worlds of imagination and discovery.

"I can't wait to get out of this cast!" Alex exclaims. "We are going to have so much fun exploring. You can be our guide." Lars responds with a smile and a nod. He is happy to finally meet pups that are his age and aren't mean like Arioch. Lars' jaw suddenly drops.

"You got hurt, right?" Lars looks back and forth between the boys. "This not done by a doctor or being sicky?" He points at Alex's leg and Tony's arm.

"Alex fell out of a tree." Tony responds. Lars crinkles his lip, looking at Tony's arm. "He landed on me." Tony continues.

"I..." Lars hesitates. The Alpha told him not to tell anyone about his powers, but surely, he didn't mean these guys. These guys are his true Alphas, anyway. At least, that's what his wolf side feels like is the case. He's a Beta wolf, and the beta's job is to protect his Alpha. He feels like he must protect these two boys, no matter what. Lars makes up his mind with a nod. "You gotta keep it a secret, but I might be able to fix you. If the wolf drain, or whatever it's called is all gone, I can make the owies go away." He looks at the boys with wide eyes and a hopeful smile.

The twins look at each other and shrug. No more hurting sounds good to both of them. "Go for it" They chorus. Lars reaches out a hand and places it on Alex's hip, above the cast. A warmth spreads down Alex's leg and instantly, Alex notices his leg no longer hurts. He can wiggle his toes without pain in his thigh and calf. Lars repeats the process on Tony's arm and chest, again, healing the boy's injuries. When Lars reaches to heal the cut on Alex's cheek, however, Alex stops him.

"Leave that. Tony and I look cool with the scars." Shrugging Lars moves his hand down. Fine by him, the scars help him tell the two apart, they look exactly alike without them.

"So, how do we get rid of the casts so we can play?" Tony asks. The three boys look at each other as the door opens.

I open the door to hear Tony asking how to get their casts off so they can go play. Looking at the three toddlers in the room, I'm met with three faces looking at me with wide grins. Alex looks at Lars, who shrugs.

"He knows." Lars says bluntly. "Might as well tell him." The boys proceed to tell me Lars healed them, begging to get their casts off so they can go exploring.

A little shocked the three-year-old thought of it, my eyes are open wide as I watch Alex try to stand with the long cast still on his leg, preventing his knee from bending. I catch him before he falls over. Giving in, I realize it's a good thing the boys aren't going to spend the summer in casts and motion for Tony and Lars to follow me while I carry Alex.

"Let's go see Doctor Hill."

By the time we reach the clinic, Alex has squirmed around to where I am basically carrying him like a football. He is pretending to fly under my arm as his brother runs circles around me. Lars looks at the scene of chaos with wide eyes, walking next to us calmly. *Orion lucky,* my wolf Blizzard mumbles in my head, *his pup not hyper.* His pup is still learning how to play, I correct my wolf. Chuckling at my wolf, I flag down the nurse and ask for Doc Hill. She leads me to a room and tells me to wait a few minutes.

"Good morning, Alpha," Doc Hill walks in as chipper as ever. "How can I help you today?" He watches the three boys giggling on the bed in the room. He takes a quick sniff of the air, probably to check if anyone's bleeding.

"Lars says he healed the boys," I point to the casts that my boys are clearly trying to get out of themselves. I pull a fidget spinner out of the cargo pocket of my pants and gently redirect Alex, who is now trying to chew his cast off like some sort of feral animal while Tony rolls around laughing at him, and Lars unsuccessfully tries to suppress his laughter. Jax will be happy to know the kid's starting to open up. He was worried Lars would be too scared to make friends.

"Really, he healed them?" Doc asks, disbelief in his voice. A low growl comes from Lars' tiny body. He doesn't seem to like Doc Hill any more than his dad does.

"Well, we'll need to do x-rays to confirm, but that's great." Doc explains that since the boys' casts are fiberglass, he can do the x-rays through them, then take them off if the bones are healed. *With how excited they are, I don't want to remove the casts before we confirm healing and risk having to hold them still to put new ones on.* Doc mind-links me his reasoning. I agree.

He grabs a wheelchair from the hall and sets both my boys in it. He asks me to wait in the room with Lars, as there is no waiting area by X-Ray he can wait in. I agreed as I needed to speak with Lars privately about using his powers. The last thing we needed was the council getting word of his powers and using him as a guinea pig. The witch Baleen may have forced him to use them for her evil experiments, but I could see the Council doing the exact same things and calling it "research for the good of the species."

"Hey Lars," I crouch down to meet his eyes as he sits in a chair far too big for him. "You're not in trouble, but I need to talk to you, okay?" His eyes widen as he looks up at me. He begins to bare his neck in submission, but I gently stop him. "No need for that, Buddy." He nods slowly and mumbles, "okay."

"Firstly, thank you for helping Alex and Tony recover. Are you enjoying spending time with them?" He nods.

"I think so. Playing with them makes me laugh. They aren't mean like Arioch. It doesn't hurt to play with them." Blizzard growls softly at the thought of Lars being hurt by a supposed playmate.

"Friends don't hurt each other on purpose," I say, looking into his eyes. "I'm glad you like them. But I need you to promise me something." He tilts his head, curious.

"You can't use your powers or shift unless it's an emergency. Only if someone's life is in danger. Understand?"

"Why? Thor needs to run too." His voice chokes up as he lowers his eyes.

"We'll arrange times for you to shift safely so Thor can run and train. But other than that, unless it's to save a life, I need you not to use your powers. There are people out there besides Baleen and the Master who might try to use you. I don't want anyone to hurt you or take you away from Jackson, Melissa, and our pack, okay?"

"Yes, Alpha," he says firmly, though still in a whisper.

"And Lars, Buddy, call me Uncle when we're not with everyone from the Pack. I'm your uncle first, Alpha second."

"Well, my 'stincts tell me Awex and Tony are my Alphas anyway."

"Hm. They will be when they turn 18. But for now, you're all still kids, okay? Just worry about having fun and growing up together." He shrugs and starts swinging his legs, smiling at me.

"Are Pa and Ma mating?" If I'd been drinking something, it would have shot out my nose. I blink and stare at him. I know Lars has seen things no three-year-old should, but sometimes he surprises me.

"Well, um, they're getting to know each other, Buddy. You shouldn't ask questions like that. It's not polite." He raises his eyebrows and widens his eyes.

"Oh. Okay."

Two toddlers come running into the room, sans casts, yelling "Daddy" at me.

"Can we go outside to play?"

"When's lunch?" The two speak over each other in their excitement. I can't even tell who asked what. It is just about lunch time, though, so I figure I'll handle that request first.

The pack house dining hall bustled with midday activity, a cacophony of voices blending with the clatter of trays and utensils. It was loud, but it was a comforting organized chaos, a simple demonstration of the Pack's unity and efficiency. I begin to enter with my entourage of tiny companions in tow. As we reach the second set of entry doors, a tiny hand grabs mine, stopping us.

"Unca." A tiny voice filled with fear whispers. Looking down, I see Lars, eyes wide, slowly inching closer to me as he takes in the scene. My pack is large and lunch is served buffet style, so it is always loud and full of movement in here. "These bad wolves or nice wolves?" He raises his eyes to me as he leans against my leg.

Tony comes over and takes Lars' hand. Alex puts his hand on Lars' shoulder, "This is our pack. They're nice wolves."

Alex smiles at Lars. "Come on, Lars. Let's go eat." Lars looks up at me, back at the boys and squares his little shoulders, taking a step forward into the room. The boys bring Lars over to the head table, where my family and Jackson traditionally eat in a place of honor as the leadership of the pack. With everything happening so quickly, there are no chairs for Melissa or Lars at the table yet. I doubt Mel or Jax are going to come down for lunch, so I settle Lars into Jax's chair. Jax's is a big guy, so his chair is larger than average, making Lars look absolutely miniature in it. Getting the boys into their chairs, I tell them to stay put while I go get them food. Eyeing one of the guards, I link him to ask him to keep an eye on the trio. Lars still eyed the chaotic room with curiosity and wariness but seemed to be more comfortable in the big chair, his occasional sniffs indicating he could scent Jax in the giant chair and was comforted by his new dad's smell as well.

With the three pups settled, I set about the task of fetching trays of food from the counters nearby. Filling three plates with chicken nuggets, carrot sticks, and mashed potatoes, I place one in front of each pup. The challenge now, however, lay not just in getting the food but in ensuring that it was consumed.

Alex and Tony dig into the nuggets eagerly, their faces lighting up with each bite. They ate their mash potatoes with glee, drizzling the ranch from the nuggets over the potatoes. The carrots, they thought they were sly and stuck them in their pockets when they thought I wasn't looking.

Lars, on the other hand, eyes his plate with a mix of confusion and hesitance. He picks up a chicken nugget with his fingers and takes a tentative bite which he smiles at, but then proceeds to use his fingers to pick up the mashed potatoes, which drip all over the table and his lap. I sigh inwardly. Jax mentioned he had difficulty with eating. "Hey Lars, let's use our fork like Alex and Tony, okay? Like this." I demonstrate how to spear a piece of chicken with a fork and bring it to his mouth.

Lars watches intently and attempts to mimic the action, his brow furrowing in concentration. After a few tries and some gentle guidance from the boys, Lars manages to successfully use the fork to eat a few bites of his potatoes. It was messy and awkward, but progress, nonetheless.

As lunch continues, I juggle between feeding bites to Lars, encouraging the twins to eat their vegetables, and responding to occasional spills and cries for more juice. The food hall around us buzzes with conversation and movement, occasional whispers reaching my ears about the messy new pup in the Beta's chair. As the boys finish eating, I wipe them all up the best I can and realize I need to address the pack. Rumors spread fast, especially when most people here can communicate with their minds.

"Attention everyone!" I call out, instantly silencing the hall. "It seems an introduction needs to be made." I pick Lars up and reassure him he is safe. Balancing him on my hip so he sees the hall and the pack sees him, "This is Lars Brousard." A rumble spreads through the hall. "He is the adopted son of Beta Jackson. Lars was rescued from rogues the other day, along with a newborn pup who is still in the infirmary. Beta Jackson also found his mate, which is why you haven't seen him today." Hoots and hollers filled the hall at that. Many packmates had been waiting for our Beta to find a mate. "We will let everyone met and congratulate the new family soon, but for now, lets welcome Lars to our pack." Anthony and Alexander are the first to attempt little baby howls and the rest of the pack shortly joins in.

I set Lars down and together, the boys gather their things and make their way to the nearby window to return their empty plates to the dish room. I hold Lars' hand as we walk, a small gesture of connection that felt significant in its simplicity.

As we leave the hall, I can't help but feel a swell of pride mixed with a touch of exhaustion. Parenting three toddlers in a bustling food hall was no small feat, but as I glanced down at the children beside me, the future leaders of my pack, I know that despite these challenges, these moments are shaping something beautiful—both for my boys and for Lars, who is slowly learning to trust in the steady presence of family.

Chapter Eight
Welcome Home

Beta Jackson

The sound of howls reverberating through the packhouse jolts me awake from my nap. For a moment, I'm disoriented, lost in the haze of sleep and the lingering euphoria of mating. My mate, Melissa, lies nestled in my arms, her soft, rhythmic snores the sweetest melody. I smile, brushing a strand of her hair away from her peaceful face, but the persistent howling pulls me from my reverie.

It takes me a moment to register the tone of the howls—celebratory, not alarmed. Relief courses through me. There's no attack or danger, but then another thought strikes me: *Luna Sara must have had her pup.* My heart races until I glance down at Melissa, still cradled against me. No, that can't be it; she hasn't left my arms. So, what's going on?

I link Alpha Len. Len's response is quick, his voice tinged with amusement. *Relax, it's good news. I introduced Lars to the pack during lunch to squash those stupid rumors. While I was at it, I let them know you found your mate. The howls are for you two—congratulations!*

Heat creeps up my neck. Well, I guess the pack is fully aware of what I've been doing the past few hours. Before I can dwell on it, Melissa stirs in my arms, her soft, perfectly rounded curves pressing against me. A low growl escapes me as her movements awaken a primal need.

Heat creeps up my neck. Well, I guess the pack is fully aware of what I've been doing the past few hours. Before I can dwell on it, Melissa stirs in my arms, her soft, perfectly rounded curves pressing against me. A low growl escapes me as her movements awaken a primal need.

Her hips shift, her cheeks brushing against my growing arousal, and my body reacts instantly. I kiss the top of her head, my lips lingering against her silky hair, and let my hand drift down her side to her hip, tracing her delicate curves. Her scent—

intoxicating and uniquely hers—wraps around me like a spell. I dip my head lower, nuzzling the mark I left on her neck. Gently, I begin to suck, my tongue teasing her sensitive skin.

Melissa moans softly, still caught in that delicious space between sleep and wakefulness. Her body responds instinctively, her hips grinding against me in a slow, sensual rhythm. I match her movements, my hand slipping between her thighs to cup her warmth. Her slick heat welcomes me as my fingers find her clit, circling it with deliberate, tender pressure.

Her moans grow louder, her body trembling in my arms as she loses herself in the moment. Her passion fuels mine, and I deepen the kiss when she captures my lips, our tongues tangling in a dance that's both fierce and tender. When her climax washes over her, her cries of pleasure are like music to my ears.

The ripple of her release sends me over the edge, and with one final thrust against her, I join her in bliss. My seed coats her thighs, mingling with her nectar on my hand. I hold her close as we ride the wave together, our breathing ragged and hearts beating in perfect sync.

I love you, Mon Chère, I whisper through the mind-link, still unable to form words aloud.

When we finally catch our breath, Melissa turns in my arms, her glowing eyes locking onto mine. Her smile is radiant, and my heart swells at the sight.

"I love you, too," she murmurs, resting her forehead against my chest. She glances up, her cheeks tinged pink. "What was all the howling about earlier?"

I chuckle, brushing my lips against her temple. "Len told the pack I found my mate." Her blush deepens, and I laugh softly. "Yeah, so they know why we weren't at lunch."

Her embarrassed giggle is utterly endearing, but I pull myself together. "As much as I'd love to stay in bed with you all day," I say, peppering kisses along her hairline, "we really should get the rooms ready for the kids. They'll need a place to come home to tonight."

She sighs, but her smile doesn't fade. "You're right." The pack storerooms are stocked with cribs, beds, and everything else a growing pup might need. It's a system that ensures no family has to buy brand-new furniture for every child, saving money and reducing waste. Melissa, ever the practical one, suggests we shower separately.

I groan inwardly, knowing she's right. A shared shower would only derail us, and getting out of bed to be responsible parents was *my* idea, after all.

Reluctantly, I press a final kiss to her lips. "Alright, but only because you're too smart for your own good," I tease, watching her with a smirk as she slips out of bed. The sight of her glowing skin and radiant smile makes it clear: the Goddess truly blessed me with this mate.

We decide to pick up Lars from Alpha Len so he can help choose furniture for his room. It feels right to let him have a say—it's his space now, and I want him to feel at home. As we approach the playground outside the packhouse, I spot

Len, Gamma Jenny, and the three boys. The twins, Tony and Alex, are no longer sporting casts and are currently racing each other up the rock wall. Lars stands at the top, looking down at them like a pint-sized king surveying his kingdom.

"Lars, that's not safe!" Melissa's voice cuts through the sounds of the playground as we draw closer.

Before I can react, Len starts waving his hands at her, clearly trying to signal her to stop, but it's too late. In the blink of an eye, my three-year-old son *jumps* off the eight-foot-tall rock wall structure.

My heart leaps into my throat, and instinct takes over. I sprint toward him, but I already know I won't make it in time. My chest tightens as I watch him hurtling toward the ground—until, with perfect grace, Lars lands in a crouch and springs to his full height like a natural-born acrobat.

Melissa gasps beside me while I fight to keep my heart from pounding out of my chest. Len chuckles and pats my shoulder. "And that's why I tried to get you to stop, Mel. If you tell a pup not to do something, they're going to do it twice."

Melissa rushes to Lars, her hands fluttering over him as she checks for injuries. But Lars tilts his head at her, his little nose wrinkling in confusion. His bright, innocent smile only adds to the surreal moment.

"I okay, Ma," he says matter-of-factly. *Ma.* He called her "Ma." My heart swells with pride and love, even as I silently wonder if I'll survive this kid's antics without turning completely grey by the time I'm thirty. He just jumped off a wall over three times his height—and landed like it was nothing.

As I wrestle with my emotions, a tiny hand slips into mine. Lars looks up at me with wide, curious eyes. "Pa, did you and Ma get to know each other this morning? Unca said you was when I asked if you was mating."

My jaw drops. My cheeks burn so hot I'm surprised I don't catch fire. Words completely fail me as I stand there, opening and closing my mouth like a fish out of water. Len, of course, is trying and failing to stifle his laughter, while Melissa watches me with barely concealed amusement.

Before I can come up with a response, Lars continues as if it's the most normal conversation in the world. "Unca took us to lunch. We had chicken pieces with brown stuff, something mushy and white I hadda use a metal stick for, and carrots. I like carrots. Tony and Awex put carrots in their shorts. Then, we come here and played. I like playing with nice pups. Are you and Ma gonna play too?"

Those puppy-dog eyes he gives me at the end are going to be my financial ruin someday, I just know it. But right now, all I can do is laugh and ruffle his hair.

"Sure thing, buddy," I say, scooping him up. His delighted giggle melts what's left of my embarrassment.

I carry him over to the swings, where the twins are already clamoring for higher pushes. "Hold the chains tight like Tony and Alex," I whisper in Lars' ear as I set him on the seat. He grips the chains with determination, and I pull him back gently before letting him swing forward.

For a while, it's just us: the boys laughing and shouting for higher swings, Len and Jenny taking turns pushing the twins, Melissa talking quietly with Luna Sara, and me pushing Lars as he squeals with joy. It's one of those rare moments of peace—no worries about rogues, pack responsibilities, or anything else. Just a couple of families enjoying a sunny afternoon at the park.

All too soon, it's time to leave. Lars protests, but when I tell him we need to get his room ready and pick out a bed, he perks up. "Can Tony and Awex come? I show them how I make a leaf nest to sleep in," he says brightly.

"We're not getting leaves, Lars," Melissa says with a laugh, though her voice has a softness to it that betrays her affection.

Lars frowns, his little face scrunching in confusion. "I sleep on the floor? No cage, though, please."

My chest tightens at his words, and I force a smile as I crouch to his level. "No cages, buddy. Never. You'll get a real bed, like the one in the infirmary—but shorter, so it's easy to climb in and out of. How's that sound?"

His face lights up, and he nods eagerly. "Shorter is good. The other bed too high. Climb down hard."

Chuckling, I pick him up again and kiss the top of his head. "Don't worry, Lars. We'll find you the perfect bed."

Melissa smiles at me, her eyes soft with understanding. For Lars, it's more than just furniture—it's safety, comfort, and a promise of the life he deserves. As we leave the park, I can't help but feel grateful for this moment, this family, and this beautiful chaos the Goddess has blessed me with.

In our mission to create an eco-friendlier lifestyle, our pack has launched an innovative furniture exchange program tailored for families with pups. It's simple but impactful: each family starts with a crib and a twin-size bed for their first pup. As the family grows, they have two options: pass the crib down to the next pup or return it to the furniture pool. From there, the pool evolves into a treasure trove of free, high-quality furniture, including twin beds, bunk beds, dressers, and just about everything a growing family could dream of. What began as a modest idea—sharing cribs—has transformed into a robust, sustainable resource, helping families thrive.

Sara and Len decided to hold on to both cribs for the twins, planning to use one for their newest addition, who Sara is expecting soon. Generously, they returned one crib to the pool, where it found a new home with us for Elizabeth. Now, we're on a mission to find the perfect furniture for Lars and Elizabeth—and it's shaping up to be quite the adventure.

Since neither Melissa nor I have much experience with pups (beyond Melissa's knowledge of newborns), Sara has joined us for this shopping trip, twins in tow. The twins, still brimming with excitement over their new race car beds, chatter enthusiastically with Lars, clearly hoping he'll pick out something equally cool. It's heartwarming to see how they instinctively recognize which pups are genuinely friendly, rather than seeking their future Alpha status. Lars, for his part, seems overjoyed just to meet pups who aren't cruel, unlike the one he was forced to endure while trapped with the Master and the witch.

When we arrive at the warehouse, Lars' eyes immediately light up. Amidst the array of donated beds, his attention zeroes in on an exquisite carved wooden frame. Made from a massive redwood branch, it still bears its natural bark beneath a protective varnish. The headboard, seemingly crafted straight from the tree trunk, exudes the calming scent of redwood sap.

"It's like having a tree indoors," Lars whispers, running his small fingers over the intricate carvings with awe.

I had intended to guide him toward one of the newer, more practical options, but I can't bring myself to dampen his wonder. His deep blue eyes sparkle with pure joy. If this bed makes him feel this alive, it's his.

The store manager explains its history: Elder Kyah had hand-carved it for his youngest pup from a giant redwood struck by lightning while his wife was pregnant. It's been in the donation pool for years, but its sheer size and weight have scared off most families. Transporting it to our apartment will involve a crane and careful planning, but I'm already committed.

"We'll take it," I say, feeling a mix of determination and excitement. We select a full-size mattress to fit the frame, one that Lars can use well into adulthood. Although he looks comically tiny next to it now, I know he'll grow into it. The mattress will be delivered first, giving us time to figure out the logistics of moving the bed frame. In the meantime, the twins help Lars pick out Mickey Mouse sheets—his only full-size character option—and we add a few sets of solid colors to mix things up.

For the rest of the room, Lars chooses a cedar dresser and a pine desk— mismatched but charming in his eyes. "They're trees. They match," he says with quiet conviction, ignoring Sara and Melissa's attempts to find something more coordinated. He also insists on a maple bookcase, reminding me that he can't yet read. His fascination with trees has me wondering if we should paint a forest mural in his room to make it feel even more like home.

Meanwhile, Sara and Melissa excitedly pick out a princess-themed nursery set for Elizabeth. The ornate crib, dresser, and rocking chair are fit for royalty, perfectly aligning with Sara's plans for her next pup, a girl named Paisley.

Once the furniture is sorted, we tackle the next challenge: clothing. Outfitting Lars proves to be an ordeal. I manage to grab a few oversized Metallica t-shirts, which he seems to love, but every pair of pants or jeans Melissa suggests is met with complaints of itchiness. After a whirlwind of trial and error, we settle on basketball shorts, cozy cotton pajamas, a stack of t-shirts, boxer shorts, and flip-flops. Shoes and socks? Absolutely not. Having spent most of his life in the forest, Lars isn't used to restrictive clothing. I can't blame him.

Elizabeth, on the other hand, is easy to shop for. Onesies and sleepers dominate her wardrobe, though Melissa can't resist adding a few frilly dresses. I bite my tongue to keep from reminding her that those dresses will likely see more baby shit than camera time. Watching Melissa's excitement over dressing a girl pup, I realize how much this moment means to her, especially after believing she'd never have pups of her own.

By the end of the day, we're exhausted but exhilarated. Lars's room is on its way to becoming a sanctuary, and Elizabeth has everything she needs to start her new life with us. It's more than furniture and clothes—it's about creating a home, one that promises safety, comfort, and love for the pups who've already endured so much.

Melissa Broussard

After we picked out the new furniture and clothes for the kids, we hustled back to the apartment to get everything settled. Jackson tackled the assembly of the furniture with his usual flair, while I dove into folding and organizing the kids' clothes. Luckily, the store had prepped everything for us, so no need for a laundry marathon. The boxers we picked for Lars are fresh and new, so no yucky surprises there.

Eager to see Lars in something other than the sweaty park gear he's been sporting; I persuade him into a fresh outfit. We're starting with baby steps in the fashion department, so I manage to swap his dirty clothes for a pair of shorts and one of the Metallica t-shirts Jackson chose. Lars might prefer running around in just his boxers, but we're on a mission to introduce him to the world of proper clothing. Tony's dapper style might just be the inspiration Lars needs.

Despite Lars' grumbling, I scrub away the dirt from his feet and legs and teach him the basics of handwashing. After a bit of negotiation—promising him cartoon time after dinner—I get him into his flip flops. He's skeptical at first, wrinkling his nose at the "squishy" feel of the flip flops. But with a bit of practice, he starts to get the hang of walking in them.

It's a milestone moment: Lars' first shoes! I'm already planning to bronze these flip flops, along with Lizzy's future regular shoes.

By the time Lars is ready, Jackson comes in, looking sharp after finishing the furniture assembly and cleaning up. "Well, my guys clean up nice," I tease. Jackson's rocking cargo shorts and a t-shirt, almost as casual as Lars, but at least he's sporting running shoes and socks.

"So, how about we grab Lizzy from the infirmary and head out for dinner?" Jackson suggests in his laid-back drawl. Lars bounces with excitement, eager to bring home the little pup he rescued. Jackson has packed the diaper bag with wipes, diapers, and bottles, but I quickly realize the diapers are too big for Lizzy and we need formula.

"We'll raid the nursery at the infirmary for preemie diapers and formula," I tell the guys. I also pack a couple of onesies for Lizzy to wear when we spring her. Attaching the car seat to the stroller ensures she'll be comfy and able to lie down since she can't sit up yet.

With everything ready, we're all set for a memorable evening. We head down to the infirmary as three fourths of our family, all of us eager to end the evening as a complete family of four.

Elizabeth is thriving—breathing steadily on her own and even sipping formula from the nurse as soon as we arrive at the nursery. Though she's still tiny, the moment has come for her to come home. I give Jax the task of emptying the bassinet's stash of diapers, wipes, and supplies into our diaper bag. As he tackles that, Lars and I make a beeline for the supply room, our mission clear: stock up on essentials for our preemie.

With my role overseeing the nursery, I know it's perfectly fine for us to take what we need. For preemie pups like Lizzy, finding the right supplies can be a real challenge. Lars and I load up the stroller with packs of tiny diapers, preemie formula cans, small bottles, and distilled water. The formula comes with a collection of baby goodies—pacifiers, burp cloths, and onesies emblazoned with the formula company's logo. I also snag a cozy little blanket from the bag, ready to keep Lizzy warm.

When we return to the nursery, we can't help but laugh. The nurse is chuckling as Jax fumbles with dressing Lizzy. She's so small she fits snugly in his large hand. Jax has managed to remove her wet diaper, and the trash can is brimming with wipes from his cleaning efforts. Now he's eyeing the tiny new diaper like it's a puzzle.

I step in to show my handsome giant the ropes, guiding him through the diapering process. Next, he wrestles with getting her arms—smaller than his fingers—into a onesie. After a bit of struggle and some assistance, he successfully dresses her and gently places her in the car seat. I demonstrate how to fasten the seatbelts and adjust them to fit her tiny form. Although a car bed would be ideal, none are available, so we make do with the car seat.

With Lizzy snug under her blanket and everything in place, we're finally set to embark on our first family meal together in the pack dining hall. The excitement is palpable, and as we head out, the promise of our new family adventure fills the air.

"She is so tiny!" Anthony's voice was filled with awe as he gazed at Lizzy in her stroller, his eyes wide and sparkling with curiosity.

"She's so pretty," Alexander chimed in, his tone soft and admiring as he took in the sight of the sleeping baby.

"She's my little pup sister. No touchy," Lars declared with a protective tone, his tiny arms crossed over his chest as he tried to assert his role as Lizzy's guardian.

"But she's just so cute," Anthony persisted, his gaze never leaving Lizzy's cherubic face.

"Like a doll," Alexander added, his voice barely above a whisper, as if speaking too loudly might wake her from her peaceful slumber.

"I wonder if Paisley will be this small," Anthony mused, his thoughts wandering to their upcoming sibling.

"Be careful! Don't break her," Lars warned, his eyes flashing with a mix of concern and authority as he kept a vigilant watch over his friends and Lizzy.

The three little boys clustered around Lizzy's stroller: their fascination palpable. Anthony and Alexander were entranced by her delicate features, watching her as if she were a precious gem. Lars, on the other hand, was like a tiny guardian angel, his eyes sharp and his posture tense, ready to leap into action at the slightest hint of mishandling.

Jax and Alpha Lenny worked to corral the boys, guiding them to their seats. The little ones were clearly reluctant to be separated from each other and the new tiny addition to the head table. Sensing their discontent, Lenny made a tactical decision, allowing all three boys to sit between me and Luna Sara, instead of his boys on one side and mine and Jax's kids on the other. I maneuvered Lizzy's stroller behind them, which seemed to soothe the miniature rebels. Even at just three years old, these kids were already asserting their authority with surprising flair.

As the kitchen staff began to serve dinner, another round of delightful chaos unfolded. Tonight's menu featured Japanese cuisine, another first for Lars, who had only used utensils on rare occasions. The kitchen had prepared a spread of dishes, including Takoyaki, Onigiri, and Udon, all of which required chopsticks. The twins had been given small, training chopsticks, and one set was brought out for Lars as well.

Despite his best efforts, Lars found himself struggling with the chopsticks. The Takoyaki and Onigiri ended up being devoured with his hands. As he attempted to tackle the Udon soup with his fingers, I swooped in just in time to prevent him from plunging his hand into the hot broth. Jax stepped in to assist, guiding Lars through the process of using chopsticks and a soup spoon.

To my surprise, Lars, despite his earlier challenges, seemed to relish the Japanese fare. When a tray of mixed sashimi arrived, he eagerly sampled various types of fish, alternating between his training chopsticks and his hands with unabashed delight.

"This is so good," Lars exclaimed with enthusiasm. "It's like eating fish from the river, but without the sticks inside!"

Anthony's eyes widened in amazement. "Dude, you eat fish straight from the river?" His tone was filled with a mix of wonder and disbelief. Anthony and Alexander had only been camping once with their dad and Jax, and their outdoor experiences were limited. Lars, by contrast, had spent most of his life living off the land.

The rest of the meal continued in a similar fashion, with Lars bravely trying foods the twins had never dared to sample. For someone accustomed to scavenging and making do with the bare minimum, tonight's dinner at the packhouse must have felt like a feast from a dream.

Once dinner was over, we made our way back to our apartment. Jax suggested a family movie night, a way to unwind and enjoy our first evening together. Lizzy finally stirred, waking up with a cry that signaled she needed a diaper change and a bottle. As I attended to her needs, Jax and Lars discussed their movie options. I had been apprehensive about whether Jax's bachelor-era DVD collection would include something suitable for a three-year-old, but my worries were quickly dispelled. Jax emerged with a copy of *Toy Story*, his face lighting up with a sheepish grin.

"The twins love it," Jax said, his smile betraying a hint of relief.

As the familiar strains of Woody and Buzz's adventure filled the room, I couldn't help but feel a wave of contentment wash over me. The night was shaping up to be a perfect ending to an eventful day, and the joy of watching our little family bond over a beloved movie was a perfect ending to our first day as a family.

Chapter Nine
There Goes My Life

Beta Jackson

Our evening unfolded like a warm night watching gators on the bayou, in other words, perfect. We had a delicious dinner, followed by the kids' first Disney movie, first movie at all, that had us all cozy on the couch as a picture-perfect family. The kids drifted off into a peaceful slumber, their tiny bodies nestled comfortably in their beds. Lizzy woke only three times throughout the night—just for a quick feed and a diaper change—before sinking back into her gentle sleep.

At the end of the night, the house was blissfully quiet, allowing my mate and me to relish some uninterrupted time together. We talked, laughed, and enjoyed each other's company, savoring the calm before the unknown storm headed our way.

As the first light of dawn sneaks through the window, tranquility evaporates in an instant. The morning erupts into a chaotic frenzy—a wild storm of energy and noise that defies any attempt at control. Lizzy's wail pierces the quiet of the house, followed by a wave of the most putrid odor I could ever imagine.

Melissa has already gone off to work, leaving me alone to handle the kids for the first time. The plan is simple: I'll take them to the mall to pick up some essentials and maybe a few toys. With Toys R Us and a variety of clothing stores, it seems like the perfect outing. But I couldn't be more wrong.

Attempting to get two kids ready on my own is utter pandemonium. Lizzy's tiny stomach is still adjusting to the preemie formula, and she wakes up engulfed in a messy disaster of runny poop that has soiled both her and her crib sheets. My huge hands fumble trying to get her tiny self in and out of clothes. They're even too big to help Lars with his clothes.

Speaking of Lars, he joins us, stumbling into Lizzy's room, drenched in sweat, his eyes shadowed with dark circles, and his nose wrinkled in disgust at the smell. When I ask how he slept, he mumbles about nightmares—visions of being back at the hands of the witch Sandia torturing him. He tells me how she would slice off his skin, showing me the scarring on his arm and leg from injuries his wolf was too weakened by wolfsbane to heal properly. Orion growls in my head at the abuse our son endured before he got to us. I make two mental notes for myself, one to let Alpha Lenny know about these additional details, the other to inflict the same damage on Sandia when we finally capture her.

I kiss the top of his head and can taste the salt from his sweat and the dirt in his hair. I realize he hasn't had a proper bath since he arrived. Lizzy needs a bath, too; there's no way wipes are going to get all the poop off her and out of her barely there hair tufts. Yup, big bad Beta Warrior, and this is my life now. Getting poop out of hair.

Time to get inventive. Both kids need baths, and there's no way I can manage them separately and safely. We didn't find a baby tub in the storerooms, so that's now on my shopping list. For the moment, I'll improvise: Lizzy will be bathed in the dish tub, while Lars can use the regular tub.

"Lars, stay with Lizzy for a few minutes while I grab what we need to get you both cleaned up," I instruct. Lars scrunches up his nose but gives a sleepy nod. I zip through the house with a sense of urgency, grabbing towels, washcloths, the dish pan, and a clean outfit for Lars. I'm back in record time, setting the dish pan into the tub and filling it with water, making sure it's just the right temperature—warm, not hot, as Melissa advised. I even manage to find some bubbles to add to the larger tub for Lars, thinking we're almost ready for bath time.

When I return to Lizzy's room, I find Lars curled up on the floor, fast asleep. My heart aches seeing him so worn out; he must be completely exhausted from everything he's been through. He's going to need extra naps. I gently wake him and help him to his feet, guiding him to the bathroom. Following his wolf instincts, Lars has been self potty trained for a while according to him, but since he peed on a decorative tree in the infirmary, we've been working on getting him to use the toilet. I have him try to pee in the toilet and see our progress when there's only a small amount of pee on the side to wipe up.

I go back to Lizzy's room to get her. I carefully wrap her snugly in her sheet to prevent spreading the mess and lay her down on a folded towel beside the tub. The soiled crib sheets and other items can wait; my priority is to get the kids clean first. The stage is set for a major showdown against the morning chaos—bubbles, warm water, and two very tired, grouchy little ones just waking up.

I help Lars out of his pajama pants; his shirt must have been lost during the night, and both his boxers and pajamas cling to him with sweat. Once he's free of his pajamas, I lift him and gently lower him into the tub, letting him sit amidst the bubbles.

"How's the water temperature? Too hot? Too cold?" I ask, my voice tinged with anxiety since this is my first time bathing a child.

"It's good," Lars replies, his eyes lighting up. "Warmer than river water, but nice." My heart sinks as I realize this might be his first indoor bath ever.

"Have you ever had a bath like this before?" I ask softly, my voice filled with a mix of curiosity and tenderness. Lars's eyes are locked on the bubbles floating on the water, his little face illuminated by a soft glow of wonder. He shakes his head slowly, his fascination evident in every bubble that pops. The simplicity of this moment hits me like a wave, and a sharp pang of sadness tugs at my heart. Lars, just barely three, has already missed out on so many of the little joys of childhood. We don't even know his birthday.

"Why don't you play with the bubbles while I get Lizzy cleaned up, okay?" I suggest gently. Lars nods eagerly, diving into his newfound adventure with a sense of discovery as he swirls his tiny hands through the frothy water. We'll pick up bath toys today, too.

Lizzy is an entirely different challenge. While Lars has grown up too fast, missing out on his baby years, Lizzy is tiny and just beginning hers. Her fragile body feels so delicate in my hands that I'm terrified of breaking her if I'm not careful. I methodically remove the soiled sheet and onesie, trying to keep the mess contained. *At least the poop isn't chunky*, I tell Orion as I pile the soiled fabrics neatly on the far corner of the towel where Lizzy lies.

With a damp washcloth, I gently clean as much of the mess off Lizzy as possible, all while bundling the soiled fabrics into the towel. Following Melissa's instructions from last night, I cradle Lizzy's head with extra care as I place her into the shallow dish pan filled with less than an inch of warm water. I work quickly but tenderly, ensuring she doesn't get cold as I wash her up and keeping the scabbing over umbilical cord stump dry. After drying her off, I wrap her snugly in a fresh towel, then diaper her and settle her next to me, cocooned in warmth.

Turning my attention back to Lars, I help him with his bath, scrubbing away the grime that's accumulated on his little body. I use the shower head to rinse him, the warm water running over him and washing away the dirt of the once feral child. When he's clean, I wrap him in a towel, making sure to dry his feet so he don't slip as he heads back into the room. I can't help but feel a sliver of hope—maybe, just maybe, I'm starting to get the hang of this Pa thing.

Or maybe not. Lars stares at the outfit I picked for him, shorts, a Metallica t-shirt, and a pair of boxers, with flip flops since he wouldn't wear any of the sneakers Mel had him try on. As he stands there, a look of confusion etched on his face, he points at the boxer shorts and asks, "Why two shorts? I pick one? Ma put shorts and pants on me last night to sleep. Lots of clothes." Whelp never thought I'd have to explain drawers to someone. "And why colorful shorts go under the pants? Why not show the mouse man shorts?" He tilts his head as he looks at the Mickey boxers and grey basketball shorts I have laid out.

"Well, I don't really know why the basketball shorts don't have designs like the boxers do." I point at each piece as I explain to him. "But people wear underwear to help be more comfortable, and to stay cleaner. It keeps the rougher seams of the shorts or pants off your private parts."

"Big people wear them?" I nod and pull the waistband of my own boxers out of the waist of my cargo shorts to show him. "Okay. Lars be like Pa." He picks up the Mickey boxers and puts both feet through one leg hole. I try to help him, and he pushes me away. "I do it."

As Lars works on fixing his boxers, I set to work getting Lizzy dressed. I slip a sun dress over her head, not too happy that the dress barely covers her diaper, but at least it shouldn't get in the way of the car seat straps. I slip her into her car seat, tuck a blanket around her over the straps like Mel told me to do and snap her seat into the stroller. Mel said to get a double stroller while we're out. We'll return this one to the storerooms, but she thinks we should have one Lars can sit in, too. Checking on Lars, I see he's managed, almost, to get himself dressed. His t-shirt is backwards and he's trying to figure out how to fix it.

"Need some help, Buddy?" with his determination to get his shorts right alone, I figure he may be working this out himself too. He's very independent when it comes to certain things, probably from living in the wild with just his wolf for so long.

"I get it," his voice comes muffled as he is twisted inside the t-shirt. I double check the diaper bag Mel packed for us last night and add some extra diapers. Mel put five in, but I add another five. I will not be caught unprepared. Grabbing a bottle, I make formula like Mel taught me and start feeding Lizzy in her stroller as Lars finishes his mission to get dressed on his own.

After picking out a double stroller and new car seats for the kids at Toys R Us, I try to interest Lars in choosing some toys. He helps me select toys for Lizzy with no problem but shows little interest in any of them for himself—until we reach the toy alligators. Lars clearly adores alligators. He picks out two stuffed alligators and about six plastic ones for himself. When I ask him why he's so captivated by alligators, he explains that they remind him of the little dragons Thor showed him when they lived in the wild. So, alligators it is. It works for me and reminds me that I'll need to take him to New Orleans one of these days to show him the swamps where I grew up.

Moving down the aisle with the plastic animals, we find a wide variety of plastic dragons. I point them out to Lars and he asks what they are.

"You said Thor showed you what Dragons look like?" He shakes his head and his eyes go fuzzy, as if his wolf is talking to him. His eyes begin to glow almost black as his wolf emerges slightly. *I showed him Asiatic Dragons, Pa. I will tell him about the Nordic Dragons one day, but those stories are too much for a young pup.* Thor links me directly. My son's eyes return to their deep blue and he picks out a couple of Nordic dragons. The display has no Asiatic dragons for him to choose from.

A few aisles over, we encounter a selection of anime toys. One that catches my boy's eye is a white, fluffy stuffed snake like toy. Reading the tag, it's a dragon called Haku, from a movie called Spirited Away.

Into the cart it goes, even though I know nothing about the movie.

After scoring a good haul of alligator and dragon toys, teddy bears for Lizzy, and some blocks and books for both kids, we move on to the clothes section. Once again, Lars is eager to pick out things for his baby sister but reluctant to choose items for himself. I have to persuade him to pick out a few more pairs of shorts; I just grab a bunch of boxers to avoid a potential argument. He does get excited about a pair of shorts with "mouse man" on them.

T-shirts are even trickier. He likes the Metallica shirts I selected but isn't fond of the truck-themed ones and other traditional boy designs on the plainer T-shirts. Knowing he'll be too small for Hot Topic clothes, I look up the Metallica store online, pick out some T-shirts from there, and eventually convince him to choose a few plain-colored ones until those arrive. Miraculously, I manage to get him to pick out a couple of pairs of pants and, shockingly, a pair of tennis shoes—though the fact that the shoes feature an alligator seems to be the only reason he agrees to wear them.

We check out from Toys R Us and head back to my truck to stow our stuff. Afterwards, we go into the mall to see if there's anything else the kids might need.

After wandering around a few stores and finding more clothes for both kids, mostly Lizzy, I decide to take a break and let Lars play in the woods themed toddler play area the mall has. I settle onto a bench along the side of the play area and tell Lars to go play.

"How?" He looks at the play area, eyebrow raised skeptically. "It looks like woods, but smells like plastic, Pa." Looking back at me, I realize, this is yet another thing we will have to teach him. How to play like a toddler. Or, how to play at all.

I can't leave Lizzy to show him, but I tell him to use his imagination and climb over the structures and pretend Jeeps in the area. One of the pretend cars is a truck that looks similar to mine. He points at it.

"I drive the Pa fruck?" he asks. Nodding my head I watch him toddle off to play for only the second time in his life. He goes to the truck and sits behind the wheel. Apparently, I need to watch myself more while driving in traffic. The next thing he does is wave his hand and say, "Get out the way, Grandma!" Mel's not gonna like that. I'll have a talk with him if he repeats it.

He repeats it. This time with some colorful words a three-year-old shouldn't know. Right when another family shows up at the play area. The mother of the other children gives me a dirty look as her children start repeating the curse word Lars used.

"Lars, come over here a second, buddy." I call to him. Tears begin to fill his eyes as the mother glares at him as he passes her. Angry at the mom for making him cry, I glare at her, then quickly soften my expression. "Hey, you're not in trouble, but there's some words you can't say, like 'shit', okay?" His little head tilts to the side.

"Why not?" he questions.

"Well, there's some words people don't like hearing, and they especially don't like hearing kids say them." He tilts his head to the other side.

"I am not a baby goat. I a wolf pup." He looks at me and blinks his dark blue eyes. I blink back at him, not quite sure how to respond.

"Okay, buddy," I start quietly, needing to remind him not to talk about shifter things in the human areas. "First, kid is another term for pup or young person, as well as a baby goat. And humans don't call their children pups, so we gotta be careful talking like that around them, okay?" He nods his head.

"Thor say no say 'shit' either. It not polite."

I decide to show him the rides, the little vehicles you put quarters in to rock. He's not very impressed, until we get to the Jeep one. That one goes a little side to side as well, and he asks to ride it three more times before I run out of quarters. After promising him we will come back and ride it another day, I decide it's time for lunch.

Chapter Ten
Should I Stay or Should I Go?

Beta Jackson

Heading to the food court, I look around at the choices. Not wanting him to eat sushi from the mall, his first choice, we opt for the Chinese place in the food court. After ordering him some noodles, we settle at a table to eat and feed Lizzy another bottle. The noodles are decent and Lars manages to get most of his food in his belly instead of on it today.

While we're eating, I notice Lars suddenly looking terrified. He slides out of his chair, moves over to me, and grabs onto my leg. "Pa, that's a bad wolf," he whispers, pointing at a man across the room. I can smell he's a wolf shifter, and he's definitely a rogue.

Lars clutches my leg, trembling with fear, tears filling his eyes. I put Lizzy down in the stroller and cover her with a blanket to keep her scent from being recognized.

She still smells slightly like her birth mother. I pick up Lars, holding him close, covering his head with my hand so the rogue can't see him. I want to go kill the rogue for scaring my boy, realizing the rogue was likely part of the horrible experience my pup had with the Master's group. Not wanting to make a scene alone in a human mall, I quickly pack up our things and move away from the food court, keeping an eye on the rogue and memorizing his appearance.

We head back to the truck, deciding we've had enough of the mall for today. I load the kids into their new car seats and stow the borrowed ones in the back. I watch carefully to ensure the rogue isn't following us. Since we're far from pack territory and I can't link Lenny, I send him a text message, letting him know we've seen one of the rogues from the master's group at the mall. Then, we head back to pack territory.

When we return to the territory, I hand the kids over to Melissa, who welcomes them with a reassuring smile, and then make my way to Alpha Lenny's office. I knock once before pushing open the door.

"Lenny, I've got a lead on one of the rogues," I say, my voice steady despite the urgency gnawing at me. I link the image of the rogue to Lenny. His eyes narrow as he takes in the details of the rogue.

Lenny's fingers fly over his keyboard, and he immediately sends out a patrol to the food court. "We need to find this guy and see if he's still there. We can't let him slip away," he says, his voice sharp with determination. The urgency in his tone reflects the gravity of the situation—we now know that the Master has sent rogues into our territory, not just lingering in the woods.

Our next steps become clear: we must prepare for a potential attack and search for the rest of the rogue group. Are they still camped out where they held Lars captive, or have they moved closer to the pack? To cover all bases, Lenny also deploys a group of warriors to patrol the perimeter of our territory, their eyes, ears and noses scanning for any signs of intrusion.

"Len, if they're getting this close, it means they are coming for my kids," I say, a knot of worry tightening in my chest.

Lenny meets my gaze, his expression softening with a fatherly empathy. "I know, Jax," he replies, his voice firm yet comforting. "We won't let any rogue get near a pup, especially not yours or mine. I promise you that." His words carry a weight of reassurance, and we exchange a quick, brotherly hug—a silent pact of mutual resolve.

With a final nod, Lenny and I head off to tackle our respective tasks, the gravity of our mission driving each step we take.

It's been a week since we saw the rogue at the mall. One week and no sign of the rogue, the Master, the witch, or any of their group. It's been quiet, too quiet. I can't shake the feeling that something is going to happen any day now. Something bad.

Which is probably why I am going over every step we took to find the rogue in my mind, visualizing every inch of the territory border we searched looking for weaknesses, trying to see if we missed anything while my beautiful mate slides her tight sheath up and down my cock. A sudden wetness on my neck alerts me to Mel whispering in my ear. Shit, all I heard was "Right?". *Orion, did you catch what Mel said?* I hope my wolf was listening. *No, boss. Uh, just moan or something.* Great, wolf's no help. I moan slightly in an affirmative "uh huh". Mel stops, my cock deep inside her. My eyes focus on her just in time for her to slap me across the cheek. *Mayday boss!* My ever so helpful wolf yelps before retreating to the back of our mind.

"Jackson Broussard! You're not paying any attention are you?"

My jaw drops in shock, "Of course I am *Mon Chére!*" I desperately try to defend myself. My love smacks me again.

"Really?" Sliding up my body, my cock slides out of her as she settles on my abdomen. "Since when do you golf?"

"What?" What in tarnation did she ask me?

"I asked you how your last golf game went. You were off in LaLa Land the last ten minutes, babe. You just hummed "uh huh" when I asked if you hit par your last golf hole."

"Shit. Mon Chére, I am so sorry. I have been stressing over the defenses ever since Lars saw that rogue at the mall. He was shaking, he was so scared. I couldn't do anything to stop the bad guy for him. The Beta in me wanted to kill that rogue for scaring my boy, but the Pa knew I couldn't fight the rogue and leave the kids alone.

"I keep feeling like we've missed something, some key point in the defenses." Pulling her down and burying my nose in her neck to breathe in her scent. Kissing her mark, I gather my strength to confess my biggest fear. "What if I can't keep them safe? What if I can't keep you safe? You're all three so much a part of me, I can't lose any of you. What if I'm not strong enough to lead our warriors to victory over the Master's Rogues?"

"You are strong enough," Mel assures me. "You're one of the best Betas this pack has ever had, and I'm not just saying that because you're my mate. I hear it from all our warriors as they come through the infirmary. I've heard of your strength and power, how good you are at your job, for years from Alpha all the way to the kitchen staff.

You stopped the rogue being a threat to Lars by removing Lars and Lizzy from the mall. You made sure the rogue didn't follow you guys back to the pack, keeping the pack safe. Without someone else there, that wasn't just the best option, it was the only option to keep the kids safe. What were you to do? Ask some random human to watch the pups while you go kill a wolf shifter rogue in the middle of the mall food court? You are good enough, better even. I trust you to keep our pack, our pups, and me safe, my love."

Kissing her gently, I mumble a soft thank you to her as I slide her hips back down my torso, rubbing my hard cock against her perfect booty. Sitting back up, she helps me guide her hips up then down to slide her tight pussy back over my cock. I lift my own hips to slowly glide into her, completely sheathing myself in her tight hole. Relishing the feel of her, I choose to live in the moment for now. Setting aside my fears, I move my hands to Mel's pert nipples, playing with them gently as I thrust into her as she rides my cock, guiding her to explode with her juices all over me.

Chapter Eleven
Symphony of Destruction

Lady Melissa

The blaring klaxon alarm pierces through the pack house, a relentless siren that shatters the tranquility of the night. Panic grips my heart as it jolts me awake, the urgent sound cutting through the fog of sleep. A cacophony of cries erupts from the nursery, mingling with the shrill alarm. Little paws patter frantically down the hallway, the unmistakable sound of Lars racing to check on his sister.

I press a swift, reassuring kiss to Jackson's forehead, my pulse racing as I leap from the bed. "I trust you," I whisper, grabbing Elizabeth's blanket and diaper bag with one arm while my other hand pushes Lars along. "I'll get Lizzy. You need to shift back to your human form and put on clothes. I bet you've ruined another pair of pajamas."

Lars, still in wolf form, shakes his head stubbornly, his dark blue eyes fixed on his sister. He bares his fangs in what seems like a snarl, though I can see the uncertainty behind his gaze. His struggle to mind-link only amplifies his frustration. "Lars, sweetheart, you need to shift. We can't let anyone know you can shift already, remember?"

His eyes convey a mix of disappointment and determination. With a reluctant nod, he bounds off to his room, returning moments later in human form. He's clad in nothing but a pair of basketball shorts and flip-flops—barely enough protection against the chaos we face. But there's no time to waste. I grab his hand, and together we dart into the hallway, where Luna Sara and her boys are also emerging from their apartment, their expressions mirroring our own anxiety.

We navigate through the corridors and head for the safe room, our steps echoing ominously against the walls. The guards, alert and ready, usher us through the hidden door to the Luna's safe room— a discreet, fortified chamber nestled between the regular pack house safe room and the storerooms.

Typically, as the Beta family, we would retreat to the regular safe room, but tonight's circumstances demand more. With Sara's due date so imminent, she must be accompanied by the pack's midwife in an emergency. Since that midwife is me, we are tasked with accompanying Sara and the boys into the fortified sanctuary. Two guards take their positions inside with us, their presence a silent testament to the seriousness of the situation.

The urgency crackles in the air as we prepare for whatever crisis awaits us. This is it. The Master and his witch have finally made their move. I'll be damned if I let them get near my kids, though. Mama Wolf is not backing down tonight.

The blaring klaxon alarm pierces through the pack house, a relentless siren that shatters the tranquility of the night.

Panic grips my heart as it jolts me awake, the urgent sound cutting through the fog of sleep. A cacophony of cries erupts from the nursery, mingling with the shrill alarm. Little paws patter frantically down the hallway, the unmistakable sound of Lars racing to check on his sister.

Melissa plants a kiss on my lips and heads to gather our pups to the safe room. My fears of a weakness somewhere in our defenses have come to fruit. Not bothering to put clothes on, I open the large window in our room, shutting it behind me as I stand on our small porch. I hear the automatic lock click into place and jump the porch railing, shifting into my red furred wolf as I do.

My warriors let me know the breach is in the same area of the woods surrounding the pack house that Lars came running from not even two weeks ago. As I begin to run to the area, Alpha Lenny's grey wolf, Blizzard flanks me on my left. We run in tandem, more of our warrior wolves joining us as we get closer to where the border patrol is fighting a large group of rogues. Blizzard and Orion immediately jump into action, each taking on a rogue within seconds of arrival. These rogues are not well trained. They fight sloppily, and not as a group.

The rogue I attack first goes down with a simple bite into his trachea. He's not dead, but he stops fighting while struggling to breathe. He seems young. Too young. The rogue shifts and a boy no more than twelve lays in its place. What the hell? I look around, several of the rogues are shifting back into teens and young boys after being taken down. These aren't warriors. They're kids. I instruct my men to subdue and detain if possible.

Some of the rogues are adults, we take those out permanently if we see them shift into adults. But the kids, no one wants to kill a pup unless we have to. Soon, we have twenty rogues who look to be between ten and sixteen detained, another fifteen of all ages lay dead among the grasses. No casualties on our side. Much to my dismay, I don't see the rogue from the mall anywhere.

I call the medical team in to treat those who need assistance healing and instruct my warriors to secure the rest to be transported to the cells. Just because they are kids and we don't want to kill them, doesn't mean we can trust them to be let go. All need to be thoroughly questioned.

The young boy I bit first motions me over after I shift and put on a pair of the shorts Gamma John is handing out. I approach him cautiously and see his wolf has healed him, but he still seems to be coughing up blood sporadically.

"The. Master... made... us, sir." He says between coughing fits. "He'll kill... little brothers... Please, help." The boy passes out and I call over one of the healers to help him.

"Get him to the infirmary and try to keep him alive." Turning to Alpha Lenny, who has also shifted back to human form, "I think these boys were forced to fight. The rogues may have their brothers held as collateral. That one" I point to the boy being carried off by a medical team "confirmed the Master forced them to fight and said he'd kill his little brothers if he didn't."

"All our brothers," another boy called out. He was about 15, restrained but sitting against a tree with tears in his eyes. I ask him to tell us what he knows. "Most of the boys at the camp are run aways, but those of us they brought here to fight, we were all pupnapped, with our brothers and sisters. I was taken from Jackson Hole Pack, some of us are from lone wolf families. That boy" he pointed to the boy I had fought first "his older sister was at the camp they brought us to before here. They're lones. The rogues took them and their two little brothers, toddlers, when they killed their parents. They've kept us at an old run-down camp about two hours from here. But all of us were taken with siblings. The girls were taken away on the first day. The older girls, teenagers, are being used by the rogues, we found out."

"Used?" I ask, hoping he doesn't mean what I think he does.

"Used." He lowers his voice. "Raped. Some of the other boys don't know yet. The one boy saw his sister being dragged into a tent. The screams were terrible, sir." The boy pauses and wipes a tear on his dirty shoulder. "I was taken with my older cousin and my little brother. They're holding my little brother, but they killed my cousin when he said he wouldn't fight. Just shot him right in the head." When the boy pauses again, I glance at Lenny. He is just as angry as I am.

"What about the younger girls?" I ask, hoping it's not the same answer.

"We don't know, sir. We haven't seen them since they split the girls into above 13 and under 13 and put them in different panel vans and drove off."

"Do you know where the camp is where they're holding your brothers?" Lenny asks the boy. He shakes his head.

"No, they had us in the back of a semi-truck the whole drive. It was mostly a straight drive, though, not many turns for a couple hours. And those grown-ups" he points to the bodies on the ground being prepared to be burned in a pit "had us blind folded for most the hike here. I might be able to remember some smells though to show you the camp where the Master and the girls are. No guarantee, though."

The safe room is cramped and dimly lit but it's clean. Bunk beds line one wall accompanied by a small crib and a larger bed against the other; between them shelves with canned goods and other needs for an extended stay are stacked neatly. The low hum of the room's only light bulb is barely audible over the distant sounds of chaos outside shouts and the occasional explosion.

Why we're hearing explosions so close I've no idea. Jackson said the fighting was near the border, not near the pack house. Regardless, I have to make sure the boys are okay and Luna Sara as well. Lars is restless. I can tell he doesn't want to be in human form. He wants to be able to protect us in his wolf form, but I don't know if Lenny has told Sara and he definitely has not told the boys that Lars can shift at such a young age. I get all three boys settled into one of the bunks so that they're together and easier to protect. I settle Lizzy into the crib. Ah to be a baby amidst the chaos. She remains fast asleep, having settled back down as soon as Lars rubbed her little foot on our way to the safe room. I know there's guards patrolling the hallway outside but in here it's just the seven of us.

Luna Sara lays on the larger bed and I notice her face is contorted in pain; damn I really hope these are just Braxton Hicks. It's my job to remain calm here. I'm the medical professional, the Ma, the auntie. I have to keep the boys calm. I need to keep myself calm.

An explosion rocks the side of the packhouse as a gush of fluid covers the bed under the Luna. Something is going incredibly wrong outside this room, but inside, we have issues, too. The Luna is about to have a baby, and since this is her second pregnancy of Alpha pups, it's likely to go fast.

We just finished restraining all the pups the rogues sent and were herding them to the cells for further interrogation and processing when explosions rang out in the vicinity of the packhouse. Shit. These kids were a distraction. Quickly directing a patrol unit to take over getting the kids to the cells, Alpha Lenny, several of our top warriors and I switched direction to the pack house.

A hole is breached in the side of the packhouse, leading into one of the game rooms for the teen pups. Alpha quickly ripped the throat from one of the rogues on the outside of the breach, while Gamma John took out the other and the rest of us entered to find the rogues inside the packhouse. Naked rogues in human form are everywhere inside the pack house. These ones are all adults. Good, I can kill adult rogues without guilt.

We break into teams, three warriors per ranked wolf. Each team takes a section of the packhouse to clear the rogues out of our home. My team heads to the basement, where our utility room and the entrances to the safe rooms are. On the way, I snap the necks of three rogues, killing them instantly and quietly.

"Mel, I don't think I can" Sara's breath hitches as another contraction hits. Yells and footsteps running can be heard outside the safe room, along with growls and howls. There's no way the warriors, Alpha or Jax are back from the border fight. Inside the halls, our junior warriors and lower ranked warriors are fighting whoever is attacking the packhouse.

Lars hops off the bed, looking between Sara, me, the twins and the door. Walking over to Luna Sara, Lars pats her hand. "They won't get through me, Wuna. I protect you and pups."

Grabbing several blankets from the shelf, Lars directs the twins to hide in the corner, on pillows he tells them to stack up with Lizzy between them surrounded by blanket rolls he makes.

"I'm scared." Anthony whimpers as he follows his probable future Beta's instructions.

"Me, too." Alex answers. Lars looks at them, determination in his eyes.

"I protect my Alphas." He assures them as he covers them with the blankets, hiding them while ensuring they can all still breathe. He looks at me, pulls off his tee-shirt and basketball shorts. Nodding at me and the Luna, he shifts into his pitch-black little wolf as loud thuds come from outside the room.

Beta Jackson

I turn the corner into the dimly lit hallway, just in time to spot a woman with cascading long hair, draped in an ankle-length black dress that flows like shadows. She raises her hand, and a swirling ball of green flames materializes, crackling with energy. With a flick of her wrist, the fireball splits into two lightning bolts, striking two warriors squarely in the chest.

191

They go sailing backward, crashing into the door of the Luna's safe room with a bone-jarring thud.

Cackling with malicious glee, the witch spins to face me. I attempt to shift, to summon my strength, but her gaze locks onto me like a vise. Instantly, I feel my body seize, as if encased in a block of ice. I can see the chaos unfolding, can breathe in the acrid scent of smoke and fear, but I am utterly immobilized. My warriors behind me remain frozen as well, their eyes wide with shock.

"Let's see if your Alpha will trade his mate for a mutt boy," she taunts, her voice dripping with menace. The air crackles with tension, and the stakes have never been higher. This must be Baleen. She clearly doesn't know Lars is in the very room she is attempting to break into.

Another flick of her wrist has my now dead warriors, their necks broken with the previous impact, suspended in the air. Her hand slices through the air and the bodies crash through the wall into the safe room. The wall tumbles, landing on and ending the lives of the two junior warriors in the safe room.

I can't believe my three-year-old is the last line of defense between the Luna, the future Alphas and a bunch of rogues, but here we are. Lars crouches in wolf form at the doorway, ready to attack any who dare enter the safe room. Thuds continue to hit the wall outside the saferoom.

"Mel," Sara calls me with a half gasp, half painful moan. "The baby is coming now." Rushing to her side, I see the baby is crowning and coming fast.

"Sara, listen to me. You're doing great. Just breathe through it." Sara grimaces in pain and squeezes my hand. At least two bones break from her shifter strength. Lenny owes me big time for that. My wolf Artemis heals it quickly so I can keep supporting Sara.

"What if the baby comes before... before this is all over?" panting, Sara looks at me, fear in her eyes. I smile at my best friend.

"Then, when the guys get here after the battle, we'll have a little surprise for Len." I chuckle at her, trying to lighten the mood. "We're prepared. I've got everything we need right here. And you're not alone. I'm right here with you."

The sound of a particularly loud thud shakes the safe room, causing the pups to jump. The fur on Lars' back stands up in spikes. Sara clutches my hand tighter, her face pale. Blood gushes onto the bed as she tears with the force of the baby coming out faster than normal.

"I can't do this" she whispers.

"Yes, you can. You're almost there. I can see the head. Just a little push and we'll have this baby in our arms." As another contraction begins, I help Sara through it, keeping my voice steady and encouraging. For once, the young alphas stay under the blankets, hidden in the corner, obeying what they are told. They must sense the gravity of the moment and huddle closer together, whispering nearly silent shushes to Lizzy, who has been woken by the thuds on the wall.

Just as the baby's shoulders slide out, Sara passes out and the wall explodes into the room, with two of our warriors' bodies flying in with the debris. All I can do is shield the baby with my body as I toss a sheet over Sara just as rogues rush into the room.

Beta Jackson

As the wall between the saferoom and the hall explodes into debris, I hear two distinct cries of infants, one female shrieking and a tiny but fierce howl. As rogues rush into the room, one slams Baleen into the floor, causing her spell on us to fall as well. Howls from all over the pack lands echo Lars' howl, telling us back up is on the way.

Jumping into the battle, I half shift, taking on the Rougarou like form most humans think of when they think of werewolves. Not all shifters can use the form, which we call the lycan form, but I happen to excel at it. My mission now is simple, protect the Luna, my mate, and the pups. I grab the first rogue I can reach. My plan is to rip its throat out, but the rogue has other plans. He shifts his hand into a clawed paw and rips down my chest. Tis but a flesh wound, though. I get my claws around his throat and squeeze, collapsing his airway and slicing open his jugular vein.

Turning to find the next rogue, I see a wolf launching at me. Just before it hits me, a tiny black bullet of fur comes flying through the air, spins and rips open the rogue's belly, spilling its intestines on the floor as it lands with a thud before me. The black ball of fur lands looking up at me with determination. *Hi Pa!* Lars chirps through the link as he rushes to take down another rogue that is approaching Luna and Melissa, who is crouched next to the bed Luna Sara is in. Melissa is holding a small bundle to her protectively. Grabbing the two closest rogues, I smash their heads together, bursting both of them. As their bodies fall to the ground, I make my way to Lars' side as he fights off any rogue that comes close to Luna, Mel, or the bundle she holds, which I am guessing is Lizzy.

Where are the twins? I link Melissa as I rip the arm off a rogue who attempts to grab Lars. Arms are too big to regrow, so he'll be out of the game soon from blood loss. He also falls, probably in shock from the rapid loss of a major body part.

Lars has them hiding in a back corner, with Elizabeth. Wait, who is she holding then? A quick glance shows blood stains around Sara, she must have had her pup. Another pup to protect in this room, along with my mate and Luna.

A scream sounds from next to me and I see another rogue fall. This one rolls on the ground as if he is trying to extinguish flames. Lars again, then. Lars takes out two more rogues by touching them and goes to crouch in front of Melissa and the bundle she holds as Alpha Lenny, who has been fighting the battle as well takes out the last rogue by slicing open its throat. Throat wounds bleed fast, so we rely on them for combat when ensuring the enemy doesn't heal and get back up is vital.

Gamma John is in the hallway, clamping iron manacles on Baleen's wrists. Iron suppresses the powers of most witches, along with a few other substances, so she won't be able to magic herself free. "Secure her in the salt cell" Alpha Lenny orders John. Salt, in high doses, also prevents a witch or wizard from using their magic. Due to the structure of the hills our packhouse is built into, we happen to have a cell made of salt floor, walls and ceiling, with an iron gate. Lenny's great grandfather took no chances when he built the prison cells here. Our torture, I mean Interrogation Room, was outstanding and I quite enjoy working in there. Can't wait to

get Baleen in there to find out where the
other kidnapped pups are being held.

Chapter Twelve
I Will Always Love You

Alpha Leonard

I order my troops to clear the bodies of the fallen rogues, the acrid scent of blood still heavy in the air. As I step into the safe room, my heart drops at the sight of my beautiful wife, Sara, lying unconscious on the bed, surrounded by a pool of crimson. Panic surges through me, and I barely register Melissa handing a bundle to Jackson before she rushes to Sara's side.

"Alpha!" Melissa's voice cuts through my fog of fear, urgent and demanding. I sprint to her side, my pulse racing. "She's lost a lot of blood. We need to get her to the infirmary, now!"

"Sara, stay with me my love." Just as I reach for her, Lars grabs her hand with surprising strength. Jackson tries to gently pull him away, but Lars stands firm, an unwavering guardian. I can see the determination in his wide eyes. Then, an unexpected warmth flares to life as a soft orange glow creeps up from Lars' tiny hand and envelops Sara.

"I fix Wuna," he declares, his voice steady despite his youth. "Protect Wuna, fix Wuna. Protect my Alphas. Always." The resolve in his words sends a rush of pride through me. As the glow engulfs Sara, she gasps and her eyes flutter open, vibrant, and alive. Relief washes over me, but my joy is short-lived as I watch Lars collapse into Jackson's arms, his small body spent from the effort.

"Wuna big hurt but be okay now," he mutters softly, fatigue draping over him like a heavy blanket. Jackson pulls him close, cradling his son, who has given us a second chance.

Melissa approaches, holding the bundle she took from Jackson, and she unveils the tiny baby nestled inside. "I told you you could do it!" she exclaims, her laughter a beacon of hope amidst the chaos. She hands the precious bundle to Sara, her movements careful and tender. "You're strong enough, love. Hold your newest pup."

Sara gently shifts the blanket, and my breath catches as I see her—our daughter. "Hello, Paisley," I whisper, the words tumbling from my lips like a vow. "I'm Daddy. You'll meet your brothers in just a moment." I glance toward the back of the room, where my boys are still hidden with Lizzy, wishing to shield the boys from the horrific aftermath of the battle. I already feel guilt weighing on me for exposing Lars to the carnage, especially since he faced many of those rogues himself.

"Hey there, Paisley," Jackson says, his voice soft with warmth.

"Heywo, Mate," my heart freezes. I snap my gaze back to the tiny creature, startled by his audacity. Does he mean "mate" as in friend, or am I going to have to lock my daughter away from my Beta's son for the next eighteen years? Does he know what mates are? I mean, his wolf might be smarter than any of us, but does Lars know what he's saying? I glance at Lars, who is utterly transfixed by my daughter, his wolf shining that unique black glow in his eyes. His head tilts slightly, absorbed in the moment as Melissa gently wipes away the bloody remnants of the battle from both him and Jackson.

As his mother releases his now-clean hand, Lars brushes his fingertip along the back of Paisley's hand with an almost reverent touch. "Boo-full, I protect, always, Mine," he whispers, a fierce declaration. To my astonishment, Paisley, whether by instinct or the bond of their spirits, wraps her tiny fingers around his.

Well, shit. This is going to be a wild ride.

The warriors gather the fallen bodies of the rogue attackers, preparing to add them to the pit we have dug for this evening's battle at the border. Regrettably, we lost four of our junior warriors—two were crushed by the wall during the chaos, while the other two perished bravely defending the main saferoom. Tomorrow night, under the full moon, we will give our fallen warriors a proper sendoff, honoring their sacrifice and valor. Thankfully, the main saferoom remains secure, and Elder Kyah has skillfully kept the pack's non-combatants calm and quiet throughout the entire conflict.

I need to uncover how the rogues discovered the precise location of my Luna's saferoom. The only entrance is a concealed door, expertly hidden from view. The warriors assigned to protect each saferoom are trained to patrol the entire corridor, ensuring no one can pinpoint the entrances. I dread the possibility of a mole within my pack. Once we have stabilized our families and the pack, I will send Jackson to interrogate the witch. He has a knack for extracting information, and I know he harbors a personal vendetta against her for what she did to Lars. While I share his anger, I will reserve my wrath for the Master. He orchestrates this chaos and eliminating him along with his leadership should put an end to the relentless kidnappings and forced servitude to his cause.

With the bodies cleared, I summon Elder Kyah to the smaller saferoom and dismiss the remaining non-combatants, instructing them to return to their homes. Meanwhile, Jackson is busy assigning patrols and implementing additional security measures for the warriors who are not involved in body disposal.

"Wait," I command, halting all warriors before Jackson can release them to their new assignments. He raises an eyebrow in response, curious about what I have to say. There is one last order I need to issue to anyone who witnessed the battle. "No warrior speaks of the small shifter to anyone. His identity must remain confidential, known only to warriors and ranked members of the pack." I use my commanding voice to ensure everyone understands the gravity of my words. I cannot shake my concern about potential leaks, nor can I risk the Council discovering Lars' abilities. If they learn he can shift and fight at his age, they may see him as a valuable asset for their twisted experiments.

As I approach Lars, I realize a conversation is necessary. He acted heroically by shifting and fighting to protect everyone, but in the future, I need him to remain in wolf form until the area is clear. While this won't completely shield his identity, minimizing the number of witnesses who see him shift from wolf to human will help protect him. Additionally, Jackson and I need to discuss how to address the concept of mates with him. It's complicated enough that a three-year-old knows who his mate is, especially when typically, a mate won't recognize their counterpart until they turn eighteen. We need to find a way to navigate this situation carefully.

As Jackson directs the warriors to their clean up and security tasks, I watch Lars and by extension Thor. Lars seems quiet, his eyes dull. Thor appears to be asleep. Looking closer, I see the light glistening of tears in his eyes.

My pup, what's wrong?

Papa Rion, I hadta kill more bad wolves. I don't like bad wolves. They mean and make me have to do bad things to them. But hadta protect Wuna, Ma, Alphas and Wizzy.

You did the right thing, pup. Sometimes we must deal with bad people in very final ways. I try to reassure him, but I am but a wolf, killing to protect our loves is in our nature. And seeing my pup near tears from having to protect our family at such a young age has my killing nature in a fury, craving the blood of every being responsible for my little pup's tears. Even if I have to declare war on every rogue who comes near our territory, I will end the Master, his witch, and anyone else who dares make my pup cry. *My boy, Papa and Pa will do everything he can to prevent you from ever needing to kill another rogue, until you are ready.*

Okay, Papa. My boy whispers to me. I tune into what Jax is doing and see he is about to meet Alpha's new pup. I sense Lars' wolf awaken just as he whispers "Hello Mate" to the newborn pup. All adult eyes in the room move to Lars.

Pup, do you know what a mate is? I asked him as Alpha let out a low growl and my human looked at him shocked. It takes him a moment to answer as he stares mesmerized at the tiny infant in Luna's arms.

Yes, Thor told me. Mate is the one I love and protect my whole life, but different than love for sister or Wuna. One day, when we grownups, mate and me be like Pa and Ma and take care of pups together. Well, pretty good for a three-year-old.

As our conversation continues, Alpha approaches Lars, kneeling down to speak with him. I tune in, eager to catch every word. "In the future," Alpha advises, his tone serious yet warm, "if you ever need to shift in an emergency, you must wait until everyone except your family and mine are gone before shifting back to your human form."

Lars nods earnestly, his eyes shining with determination. "I understand," he responds, a grin breaking across his face. "I actually prefer my wolf form sometimes anyway! It's how I was born." Alpha chuckles at him. His innocent confidence fills me with pride as I watch the bond between him and our Alpha grow stronger. Alpha is his uncle, after all, both as Jackson's best friend, and as Kade's foster-brother, they should have a relationship like Jackson and I share with Alpha Lenny's boys.

Alpha leaned closer to Lars, curiosity dancing in his eyes. "What do you mean when you call Paisley 'mate'?" he asked.

Lars looks at Paisley with adoration in his eyes. "She my mate, mine. I love and protect her for all our lives." Alpha pressed for more details, eager to understand.

"How do you know she's your mate?"

"Smell like rain through big red bark tree. When I touch her baby paw, er hand, I feel little tingles. And Thor said she is our mate." His eyes sparkled with certainty, revealing a bond deeper than words could express.

Alpha tilts his head, blinking at my pup. With that description, there's no question Paisley is Lars' mate. The question is, how do we ensure Paisley gets the same experience feeling the mate bond the first time. Alpha takes a deep breath and lets it out slowly. Looking around at Melissa, Jackson, Luna Sara and then back to Lars, he nods.

"Lars, I can't and won't take away your knowledge of who your mate is. However, I can protect her and allow her to experience the realization of the bond when she is destined to, probably after she turns eighteen like most shifters. I command you, Lars Brousard, not to tell anyone except your mother and father, Luna Sara, and I that you know who your mate is or who your mate is until said mate recognizes the bond herself. I further command the adults in this room not to speak of Lars' mate bond with anyone not already having the knowledge of the bond." A jolt of power spreads through the room as the command was sealed.

"Yes, Alpha Leonard," a chorus of voices acknowledge the command, binding us to obey it. A shifter cannot go against the command of their alpha.

Alpha Lenny ordered us not to talk about my three-year-old's mate. Sheesh, my three-year-old officially knows who he will date, mate, and have pups with. This is like a human knowing who they will marry at three. I can't even imagine how Lenny feels, having his newborn daughter already having a mate. I'd be ticked if the twins claimed Lizzy as their mate at this age, so Len is handling it better than I would.

Speaking of the twins, the warriors finally have all the bodies and prisoners secured and Lenny is now introducing them to their new sister. Mel holds Lizzy, who the boys say slept right up until the warriors' bodies flew through the wall. Alex says she calmed down when he held her and Tony rubbed her back.

All the kids are exhausted, and Luna Sara needs rest to finish healing, so we leave the final clean up and repairs to our construction crew and head to our respective apartments to get the kids back in bed. I want to head straight to the cells to interrogate the witch, but as Lenny said she will be there in the morning.

Chapter Thirteen
Dark Side

Beta Jackson

By the time I wake up in the morning, the sun is nearly at the peak of the sky. I definitely missed the morning training session and technically am late for work. Mel is already up with the kids, who sound grumpy. I pull on some shorts, do my business in the bathroom real quick like and head to Lars' room, where the grumpy voices are coming from.

"Why I hafta wear the itchy shorts?" a frustrated cry meets my ears as I head down the hall. "Why can't I wear the soft boo shorts?" My wonderfully patient mate explains the "boo" or blue shorts are sweat shorts, and not appropriate to wear to school. Oh, man, Lars' starts preschool this afternoon and Lizzy has her first daycare day. With the battle last night, it totally slipped my mind. Off to help my mate with a different kind of battle, helping get my pups ready to go.

After an unexpectedly uneventful drop off at the preschool and daycare, I find myself outside the entrance to the dungeon to start what looks to be a great day at work. I have a beast inside me and I don't mean Orion. As a Beta, it's in my blood to protect the weaker members of a pack, and society. I find when it comes to my family and children, that protective instinct is a beast who is waiting to take revenge on all those who hurt my sister and my pup.

Following the steps deep underground, the smells of the dungeon begin to hit my senses. The metallic, rusted penny smell of blood, the stench of rotting flesh and feces, mixed with urine. The sounds of prisoners moaning and screams. All warfare ends with prisoners, supernatural war is no exception. After years of waiting, we finally have one of the leaders of the evil group of rogues in our custody. And, to both Orion's and my joy, the bitch we had come to know as Sandia Baleen was the one. After hearing what she had done to Lars, and other pups and she wolves, Orion and I thought she might be even worse than Piers Jameson, the wolf shifter that calls himself the Master.

I continue to the salted room at the end of the dungeon, where the warriors have informed me Baleen is secured in iron chains. Entering the room and I see she is bound to the chair, with leather and silver straps in addition to the iron chains, a circle of additional salt surrounding her so she cannot leave, physically or with magic. Another ring of salt surrounds the edges of the room, an extra layer of protection against escape. I make a mental note to thank Gamma John for that. I'm pretty sure the first circle of salt is about to be broken with my plans and Sandia's blood. She's already got blood running down the side of her head, whether from the battle or

John and the warriors tying her up, I don't know. Actually, I don't care.

I approach the wall of herbs and tools designated for interrogating supernaturals. Every supernatural being has some herb, metal, or substance to which they are vulnerable, and this room stocks a variety of them. The more dangerous items, like wolfsbane, are secured in a locked cabinet. But Sandia is a witch; without access to her magic, she becomes as weak and fragile as a regular human.

As I prepare my tools on a cart, I hum "The Thing That Should Not Be." I toss rubbing alcohol, gauze rolls, and salt onto the cart, then begin browsing the herbs. I grab basil, bay leaves, and sandalwood, along with a sturdy pestle and mortar. While passing by the shelves of tools, I select a whip lined with silver barbs. Though silver doesn't harm witches as it does wolves, the sharp barbs promise pain. Lars described how Sandia and her rogue companions used a similar whip, soaked in wolfsbane, on him. It feels fitting for the revenge I intend to extract.

I also grab a hammer and a knife, choosing not to bother with a silver blade, yet. I can't resist smirking at Sandia as I pick up a cheese slicer. She often used a knife to slice chunks of flesh from Lars for her so-called experiments, but I decide to take my time, ensuring I remove every piece of her flesh. Dark? Yes. But this witch is pure evil. Based on Lars and the surviving youth warriors' descriptions, Sandia will experience all the pain she inflicted on those pups tenfold, especially what she did to my boy. It's tragic she cannot heal like a wolf. If she could, I would stretch this out even longer. Alas, once I dampen her magic, she will be nothing more than a human—and she won't survive the next forty-eight hours, tops.

Throughout my selection of tools and herbs, Sandia's eyes follow me, filled with growing dread. When I pull the sandalwood off the shelf, I see terror flicker in her gaze. She knows exactly what I plan to do. I learned this little bit of magic as a teenager, spending summers at my grandfather's pack in New Orleans. That city pulses with magic and supernatural energy, so much that even humans sense it. They call it the most haunted city in the country, where spirits become trapped in the high levels of supernatural energy. Voodoo priestesses, witches, and various shifters make the area their home. My grandfather, the former Alpha of the Acadian Pack, instilled in me the importance of defending against hostile supernaturals. Now, I prepare to brew a poultice and potion designed to destroy Sandia Baleen's magic—and it will hurt.

I start with the poultice, grinding salt and basil together, adding a splash of alcohol to form a thick paste. Grabbing Sandia's hand roughly, I slice a piece of flesh from her palm with the cheese slicer, spreading the paste over the wound and wrapping it tightly with gauze. I repeat the process on her other hand. As the poultice begins to work, I watch her clench her teeth, the stubborn witch trying not to scream. That resolve won't last long.

I hold back from completely stripping her powers just yet; I want to savor my revenge. Plus, the poultice needs time to rest for full effectiveness. I ignite a fire in the pit we use to heat our tools. Some supernaturals only weaken under red-hot instruments. Once the flames crackle to life, I toss the two pieces of Sandia's flesh into it, ensuring a clean workspace.

I grab a cast iron pot from the shelf, pour in some alcohol, and set it over the flames. I add sandalwood and bay leaves, allowing the mixture to simmer and release its potent aroma.

"So, Sandia," I begin, my voice steady. I need information from her. We must locate Bonfare and Jameson's hideout for the kidnapped pups. "Are you ready to share where the pups are?"

"What pups?" she hisses, her eyes glowing a dull pinkish red. Ah, such fight in this witch. She still thinks she has a chance.

"Well, now." I smirk, savoring the moment. "I guess this is going to be more fun than I anticipated." I grasp the back of the chair and fold it down on the hinges Leonard installed for this very purpose. The chair allows access to a suspect's back without the need to untie them. Our pack is feared for our ability to break those we interrogate; our methods are infamous in the supernatural world. Those who survive often wish they hadn't. We prefer peace, but we are animals at our core, and we have no problem inflicting pain or death when necessary.

Sandia Baleen has only just begun to feel my wrath. She brutally abused she wolves and pups in her twisted attempts to create forced hybrids, and she is part of the group that killed my sister and friend while tormenting my own pup as a baby. She will feel pain before she dies, and with luck, I'll uncover where the missing pups are hidden. I pick up the silver-tipped whip, careful not to touch the razor-sharp barbs. I dangle it in front of her, and her eyes widen in fear.

"I'm not a wolf, mutt," she spits at me, though I can smell the fear radiating off her. I glare back, unyielding. "Silver won't kill me," she adds, her confidence wavering.

"Oh, it won't kill you," I chuckle lowly. "But it will hurt, and you will bleed." Her eyes grow wide as I growl the last sentence, now faded to a pale pink. The poultice begins to take effect; her magic remains, but she can't draw on it. Good. Very good.

"Let's see...my pup has at least thirty scars on his back from you monsters whipping him," Orion growls, surfacing with anger over what they did to Lars. He refrains from using his name; he won't give this witch the satisfaction of knowing it. "Maybe we start with that. Anytime you want a break, you can tell me something useful."

I lift the whip, pausing to watch her, waiting for her to beg for mercy while keeping her uncertain about when the blow will come. I bring the whip down across her back, relishing the sound of her scream. I knew she couldn't hold back for long. As I prepare for a second strike, I hear the distinct bubbling of the potion in the pot. Ah, time to add some salt. Like we Cajuns always say, proper seasoning is a must.

I toss the salt into the simmering concoction, lifting it off the flames to rest. I still have extra salt in my hand. With a smirk, I sprinkle it onto the open wounds on Baleen's back, rubbing my hands together to shake off the grains. She shrieks in agony as the salt burns into the cuts from the whip. "Waste not," I chuckle, picking the whip back up.

"Wait! I can tell you where the boys are trained! Well, the area. Piers never let me see exactly, but I know the general vicinity from the protection spell," she cries out, desperation creeping into her voice. I know I can't fully trust her, even under duress; she is still a witch, nearly as untrustworthy as a vampire.

"Where?" I growl, my voice low and menacing. "Maybe I'll spare your life if the information pans out." I have no intention of sparing her life, but I relish giving my victims a glimmer of hope. It makes breaking them all the more satisfying.

The witch smirks at me defiantly. I twirl the whip handle between my fingers, enjoying the tension in the air. "I'm waiting," I growl, tilting my head slightly at her. That smirk won't last long.

"Between Alfred's Church where crows attack and George's former dark side ranch. From salty seas to where false evil turns to breeze. That's where you'll find the pups with fleas."

"The fuck?" I draw the whip through the air, slicing through her back again. "What kind of nonsense is that bitch?" She begins to alternate between cries of pain and evil cackles. Two more strikes with the whip have her cackles dying out.

Setting down the whip, I ask her again where the kidnapped pups are. All she responds is the nonsensical rhyme over and over. The potion that will take her magic permanently needs more time to simmer, so I decide to switch tactics to find out where the pups are being held.

"You will tell me where the other pups are being kept." I pick up my hammer, place her hand on the flat surface of the armrest and bring the hammer down quickly on her knuckles, crushing them into mush. Her painful scream is satisfying, but not as much as knowing where the camp would be. She refuses to tell me where the pups are, not even a general location, just repeating the nonsense poem.

After smashing each of the bones in both of her hands, still without a clear answer to where the pups are, I decide to switch my questioning to find out everything she did to Lars. I would come to wish I hadn't. Her lack of answers at first is frustrating, so I switch to a drastic measure.

Taking the bottle of sodium hydroxide from the shelf, and a small bucket from the cabinet, I prepare for the next level of torture. I don thick gloves to protect my own hands and set the bucket on a small stool next to Baleen's chair. Loosening the restraints on her hand just enough, I place her hand in the bucket and re-secure the chains so she cannot move her hand again. Soon, she won't have a hand to move. I place a bottle of Sulfuric acid where she can see it, and slowly pour the sodium hydroxide over her hand. I can smell her skin burning as she screams in pain.

"Start talking. Tell me everything you did to the toddler shifter your camp held and I'll neutralize the chemicals burning you." I wiggle the bottle of acid in front of her tauntingly. Apparently, dissolving one's hand off while they live is enough to get them to talk.

Baleen devolves into a horrific tale of how she removed flesh from various areas of Lars' little body, especially his palms, in attempt to find how he can burn things with his hands. His blood was drawn to inject into pregnant she wolves to attempt to make their pups early shifters. Other experiments hoped to make pups with Lars' ability to control fire in his hands. All appeared to be unsuccessful.

Some of the worst things that were done to Lars at the camp weren't done by Baleen, though. Jameson, the wolf who fashioned himself the Master, would force Lars to allow his son, Arioch, to beat him. Jameson called this "training" for Arioch to learn to fight, even though Lars was not allowed to fight back or defend himself. If Lars did attempt to defend or fight back, Jameson would beat him.

Bonfare, the human scientist Jameson and Baleen worked with was even more cruel. He forced Lars to use his ability to internally burn things to kill the young and newborn pups experimented on that were deemed failures. Baleen and Bonfare would make him burn newborn pups to death, under threat of more beatings and pain. Hearing the horrors my pup was forced to endure at such a young age outraged me.

I forgo neutralizing the sodium hydroxide, allowing it to continue to dissolve Baleen's hand. Only when the bones began to fall to the bottom of the bucket, do I toss the acid over her stump to stop the burning. And only then because the burning flesh smells bad.

The potion that will permanently eliminate Baleen's magic is finally ready. I strain the potion into a small bowl, separating the moist leaves that remain into another bowl. Drawing a full 10mL syringe of the potion, I inject it into Baleen's jugular vein, savoring her screams as it entered her system, burning the vein walls as it traveled to her heart. As the potion pumps through her arteries to her entire body, it will burn and destroy the cells that hold the witch's magical ability in her body. For good measure, I draw up another 10mL, inject it, and cover the injection site with the moist leaves strained from the potion. It will take some time to work completely, so I decide it's time to go check on my kids at the daycare and preschool. Looking down, I realize I need to shower first.

Chapter Fourteen
Brightside

Beta Jackson

The shower room in the dungeon lacks any clothing that might fit me. In my rush to reunite with my family, I completely overlook the need to check for suitable attire before stepping into the stark, utilitarian shower fully clothed. Now, I stand there, drenched, and frustrated, searching for a towel that doesn't exist. Why is this room so poorly stocked? I mentally note that I'll need to confront the guards about this oversight later. For now, I face an embarrassing choice: walk to my quarters soaking wet or go in my birthday suit. Given that I want to avoid Mel's wrath affecting any she wolf I may pass on the way to my quarters staying wet seems like the better option.

As I push open the door to my quarters, a familiar and intoxicating scent envelops me. It's Mel, the most beautiful she wolf in the world, and I can't help but smile despite my predicament.

"Why do you smell like another female?" Her voice slices through the air, sharp and accusatory, as she steps into view. The tension in the room thickens as her fangs begin to descend, glinting menacingly in the dim light. "Wait—why are you covered in blood? I can smell it's not your blood. There was no battle today, and you weren't at training, according to Gamma John. He mentioned you weren't there at all; he brought in one of the junior warriors for a cast."

Her eyes flash with a tumultuous mix of suspicion and concern, and I realize I need to explain myself quickly. Taking a deep breath, I try to calm the storm brewing behind her steely hazel gaze.

"Mon Chére, I was interrogating the witch," I say, extending my hands slightly, hoping she'll see the sincerity in my eyes. The weight of her past experiences hangs heavily between us—the false stereotypes about playboy betas are probably not helping her mood right now. Her *couillion* ex-mate, also a beta, betrayed her before rejecting her. "My love, you are my one and only, *mon seul et unique, âme sœur,* my soulmate."

I slowly reach my arms out, ready to wrap her in a comforting embrace, but she halts me, recoiling as if I'm a flame she's afraid to touch. Panic flares within me; I need to find a way to prove my innocence. Just as I'm about to call for the guards who saw me head into the dungeon to back me up, she cuts through my thoughts.

"Shower, my love. Then hugs. You're covered in blood." Her playful, seductive smile teases at the corners of her lips, and suddenly I realize I might be in for more than just hugs if I hurry. Tossing my blood-soaked clothes into the trash, I leap into the shower, not caring that the water is barely warm yet.

The witch's blood swirls down the drain, mingling with the remnants of the dungeon's grime. I lather up with the disinfectant soap I keep on hand for these occasions, scrubbing vigorously until the water runs clear. The heat of the water washes over me, soothing my tense muscles, and I grab the shampoo, indulging in a fragrant escape.

As I close my eyes, ready to rinse away the last of the day's chaos, the shower door swings open, flooding the small space with the tantalizing aroma of daiquiris. Two tiny but powerful arms wrap around my waist, pulling me back into a warm embrace. Soft kisses pepper my chest—my little mate.

"Looks like I'm not the only one needing a refresh," I tease, turning to meet her gaze. Her eyes sparkle with mischief, and I can't help but smile, feeling the tension dissipate. Wrapping one arm under her perfect booty and one around her back, I lift her so her lips meet mine. Kissing her between words I promise her "You are the perfect little snack, but I'm going to make a meal of you."

Lifting her even higher, she wraps her legs around my shoulders, leaning against the shower wall for balance. "Jackson" she shrieks, clinging to me tightly.

"Oh, *Mon Petite Chère*, I love when you call out my name." Slipping my tongue between her folds, I slowly run my tongue down to her center then just as slowly back up to her clit. Warm water cascades down our bodies as I circle her clit then dip my tongue into her cavern, pumping in an out of her, licking the special spot inside I know will make her explode for me. I slide my arm from around her back to wrap around her strong thigh. Dampening my thumb with her juices, I begin to circle her clit with the pad of my thumb, not slowing my ministrations on her cavern one bit.

She thrusts both hands into my hair, lightly tugging at it. Her head tilts back as I work my tongue rougher and faster against that special spot in her cavern. She moans out my name just before she explodes with her orgasm, coating my goatee and mustache with her juices. Kissing her clit as she comes down from her high, I whisper to her *"mon seul et unique, âme sœur."*

Mel moves her legs to wrap around my waist and rests her head on my shoulder, panting as she attempts to regain control over her breath. Once she catches her breath, I set her on her feet, marveling at her perfect body, so small and delicate compared to mine.

I begin to walk her backwards, out of the shower toward our bed. The sudden chirping of our cell phones interrupts our walk. My phone is ringing the tone I set for the daycare. Simultaneously, feelings of frustration and worry enter my soul, both mine and Melissa's. I quickly answer my phone.

"Beta Jackson, we need you to come pick-up Lars." Shit, what happened? Responding I'm on my way, I quickly hang up my phone and look at Melissa, who is already getting dressed.

"You a shithead!" Lars' voice cuts through the air as we walk into the daycare, a chaotic scene unfolding before us.

"No take toy from baby!" Anthony yells, standing tall with his fists clenched.

"It was sittin' there!" a tow-headed pup argues, her face scrunched in frustration.

"No take!" Alex adds, his voice sharp and angry.

The three little boys stand in a defensive formation, their small bodies rigid as they face off against a single pup—one I don't recognize. The boys are blocking the way of a crying Elizabeth, who's being held by one of the daycare workers, struggling to calm her down as the workers try—and fail—to break up the squabble.

I'm not usually involved with the pups of this age; I tend to leave that to Lenny, who's better suited for the job. But as I step into the room and see Lizzy's distress, my parental instincts flare. Inhaling deeply to center myself, I'm about to give the pups a command to stop when I feel the familiar, powerful pulse of Alpha energy rush through me. From behind me, a voice booms, resonating with the authority of Alpha power, "Silence."

The room immediately stills. Every pup falls quiet—except for Lizzy, of course. As always, even an Alpha's command can't calm the cries of a newborn.

"First off," Lenny says, his voice calm but firm, turning his attention to Lars.

"No swearing. 'Shit' is not a word for little boys to use." He pauses and surveys the room, the energy in the air still crackling with tension. "Miss Phyllis, what happened here? And pups, no interrupting while she explains."

Phyllis, a seasoned worker who's usually on top of these things, looks at me with wide eyes before handing Elizabeth into my arms. The instant Lizzy is with me, she settles, her cries tapering off as I hold her close.

"I was changing a diaper on another pup when Elizabeth started crying," Phyllis explains, her voice steady despite the chaos around us. "I turned around to find Lars, Anthony, and Alexander pulling the bear from Gretchen's hands and yelling at her."

I immediately recognize the bear— Lars picked it out for Lizzy at the toy store. It's one she's been sleeping with for a week. It's hers. I nod, confirming to Lenny that it's definitely Lizzy's bear.

Phyllis continues, "They haven't stopped yelling at Gretchen since."

Lenny turns his attention to the three boys. "Anthony, Alex," he says, addressing the inseparable pair, "I know you won't talk unless you're both involved. Tell me what happened."

Anthony steps forward first, eager to explain. "The bear is Izzy's," he starts, his voice defensive but earnest. "She brought it from home."

Lenny looks at me, and I nod again to confirm. Yes, it's Elizabeth's bear, no question.

"Wretchen take bear toy from Izzy," Alex chimes in, his small face serious as he points an accusing finger at Gretchen, the unfamiliar pup standing at the edge of the group.

"She no give it back when we ask, so we take it," Anthony adds, his voice rising in frustration as if it's the only reasonable course of action.

"It Izzy's," Lars interrupts, clutching the bear even tighter, as if to ensure no one could dispute his claim. "I pick it for her at the toy place!" He looks so proud, his chest puffed out, as though his act of picking out the bear somehow made him the ultimate authority on it.

Lenny nods, processing the situation, then turns his gaze toward little Gretchen. "Gretchen?" he asks, his tone softer but no less commanding.

Gretchen freezes, clearly intimidated by the Alpha's attention. She shifts her weight nervously, looking down at the floor. "It sittin' there," she begins hesitantly, "I thought it school toy."

The moment her words leave her mouth, the boys growl, a low, collective sound of warning.

Lenny raises an eyebrow, unimpressed by her excuse. "Is that so?" he asks. "Let's try that again, Gretchen. What really happened?"

Gretchen squirms, realizing she's been caught in a lie. With a resigned sigh, she confesses, "I take it from Izzy's bouncy chair... It next ta her, and I want to pway with it."

At that exact moment, the door to the daycare opens, and in walks Gretchen's mother, Regina. The air shifts immediately, the weight of her presence hanging heavily over the room.

Regina's known around the pack for her... colorful history. She didn't wait for her mate and, as whispers go, Gretchen's father is human—a detail that always seems to cause more tension than necessary. On top of that, Regina has had questionable relationships with several unmated males in the pack, possibly a couple who were mated, too. I can't help but feel a pang of sympathy for Gretchen—she doesn't deserve the complicated mess of her mother's choices. But that doesn't change the fact that she can't just take Lizzy's bear.

Lenny assesses the situation with the efficiency I've come to expect from him. Lars is still holding the bear like it's the last thing he'll ever own, his tiny hands gripping it with fierce possessiveness. The Alpha twins stand rigid at his side, glaring at Gretchen like they're ready to pounce.

"Alright," Lenny says, his voice ringing with finality. "All five pups are going home with their parents today. Gretchen will be moved to the other daycare site, effective tomorrow."

Regina opens her mouth to protest, her face contorting in disbelief. "Wait, what? The other daycare is on the other side of the pack! That's... that's ridiculous!"

Lenny cuts her off before she can go further, his tone unwavering. "No arguments, Regina. She's been here full-time because you need to find work outside the pack. But after alienating every department head, the situation needs to change."

Regina falls silent, her mouth snapping shut with a quiet snap, her frustration palpable.

Lenny turns his attention back to Lars. "Lars, once again, we've talked about language. 'Shit' isn't a word for little pups. Your Pa can explain it to you later, alright?"

Lars hangs his head in response, muttering a soft apology, though I can tell he doesn't quite understand why it's wrong yet.

Lenny shifts his focus to his own sons. "You two will play quietly in the playroom by my office until I'm done at work. Mama still needs her rest, so you're with me today."

The room seems to exhale in relief as the tension starts to dissipate. I look down at Elizabeth, her small body tucked safely in my arms, her cries finally quieting as she calms into the comfort of my embrace. It's been a long day, and I know there's still work to be done in the dungeons. But for now, at least, I get to focus on my family. My mate. My pups.

Chapter Fifteen
2x4

Gamma John

The sun sets, casting long shadows over the jagged landscape. I crouch low behind a craggy outcrop, the rough stone cold against my palms. I can hear the pounding heartbeat of the boy who lead us here. I force my breath to steady, motioning him to match me and the rhythm of the world around us. The Master's camp lies just beyond the ridge, a collection of flickering fires and large tents, vague shapes moving in and out of the dusky light and faint cries.

We've been watching for hours now, tracking their movements, noting every shift in the guards' patrols, every whisper of activity that might give us clues. The Master's troops move with practiced ease—too well for a ragtag group of rogues. These men know what they're doing. I see them gather around the fire, laughing, drinking.

But it's not their drunken jeers I care about. It's what they're hiding, somewhere in that maze of tents and huts.

There were rumors, of course. The whispers that made it back to our pack. Pups taken in raids, dragged away to be sold or worse. Missing runaways, Alphas losing track of lone wolf families that lived near their packs. But wolves don't speak of them openly. No. Not until Beta found those two little ones the other day.

A warrior steps into the dim light near the entrance to a larger tent. He's holding something, a bundle, but it's too far to make out. My eyes narrow, my hand tingling, itching to shift and attack this scum. There's something about the way he clutches it; the careful movements that tell me this isn't a simple bag of supplies.

Another figure appears beside him— a human, sharp-eyed, a grim set to his mouth. He doesn't look like the others. He's not drunk, and his posture is stiff, like he's in charge. I watch them exchange words, too far away to catch, even with my enhanced wolf hearing. But then, the human looks in the bundle and nods, shifting the cloth just enough for me to see the contents. A child, baby probably. The warrior tucks the bundle under his arm, his gaze scanning the camp for a moment before he disappears into the darkness beyond.

My pulse quickens. That's it. The pups and girls are here, hidden among them. Somewhere in that sea of tents, those cursed monsters have them. The human's eyes lingered over the camp for too long— he was scouting, checking for anyone who might have seen him. There's a passageway through the east side of the camp, a hole in the bushes barely wide enough to crawl through, where the shadows deepen. I make a note of it, counting the seconds in my head, mapping an escape route.

We watch for another hour, noting where the guards change shifts and where the firelight doesn't reach. I don't trust the darkness, but I know how to use it. I can slip through this camp undetected. I just need to find them. The girls, and any newborn pups we can save.

As the night draws on, I send my warriors back to the pack with the young boy and instructions to report what we've found already to the Alpha, but I don't move. I won't leave this spot until I know exactly where they've hidden those children. Until I know that when I act, I can bring them to safety.

Beta Jackson

Since I still have work to do in the dungeons, a place I certainly don't want to bring Lars and Lizzy, I meet up with Melissa to drop the kids off with her. Upon my return to the dungeon, screaming, both in pain and with spells can be heard through the halls. It's Baleen. I'll be stopping that soon enough.

With no time left to continue torturing Baleen, though she deserves it for everything she has done to the women and pups at Jameson's camp, it's time to take care of our witchy problem. There will be no whips or potions this time, no taking my time to exact revenge for my pup and all the other pups and she wolves harmed by this trash. I walk in the cell with the pack's *special* knife. We may not clean it, but we sure do keep it sharp. It will do nicely for this.

Baleen is screaming, rambling out spells that won't work coming from her powerless core. She must know what I've come back to do. The one way to effectively kill a witch. I raise my blade and slice it through the air in front of me as I look into her eyes. This witch will never harm another.

"For Lars."

Her head falls to the floor and rolls toward the cell wall, bounding a little as her nose hits the floor, altering the pattern of the roll. Not wanting to waste any time, I walk over and stop it, placing it in the cauldron I previously brewed the potion in. Calling in a guard for help, I begin undoing the chains and restraints holding her dead carcass on the chair.

Witches must be beheaded, then their bodies burnt to ashes, with the head burnt separately, to ensure they are truly dead.

The guard carries the body to our cremation chamber, while I carry the head to our dungeon fire pit. We load the body into the cremation chamber. Despite Baleen having no magic left, I am leaving nothing to chance. I am going to ensure she never harms another.

Deciding to be absolutely certain she will pay for her crimes; I chant a little voodoo spell Gram taught me that will ensure her soul burns in the afterlife. Then, we load the body into the cremation chamber. I lock the door with the regular lock out lock, adding another lock only I have the key to. No one will be able to stop this cremation. Turning on the gas flames of the chamber, I watch as my pup's tormentor begins to burn. I won't expose him to this image, but hopefully my words will be enough to ensure him she is dead and gone, slowing his nightmares so he can grow up a regular pup. Or, as regular as a part dragon pup with fire and healing powers that can shift at three years old can.

Turning to the fire pit, I light it and wait for the flames to burn hot enough for the head to burn. Since it will take a few minutes, I send the guard to grab some hydrochloric acid. The head will burn faster if I dissolve the flesh from the bone. Or even some flesh. For once in my career as Beta, the head enforcer and executor of the pack, among other duties, I would rather be home instead of working. Interesting.

Once the flames in the fit pit are hot enough, enhanced to burn hotter than normal for the redwood 2x4 scraps we use for these body disposals, I toss the remains of the skull, bone, and flesh, into the pit. Colorless flames rise from the pit as the formaldehyde burns off the skull, then light green flames as her witchy flesh begins to burn. Had I not stripped her powers, it would be a brilliant florescent green light. I stand there for an hour, ensuring every bit of skull and redwood kindling turns to dust.

Time for another shower and to return to my family.

The moon is a mere sliver in the sky, and the night is thick with the scent of damp earth and smoke. I crouch low in the shadow of a thick cluster of trees, my eyes fixed on the camp ahead. The flickering light of campfires dances between the tents, casting long shadows across the rough ground. The Master's camp is a disorganized mess, but there's a chilling order beneath the chaos—a kind of twisted efficiency.

I've been watching them for hours now, tracking their movements, learning their routines. The soldiers are careless, drunk on their own sense of power, but I know better than to underestimate them. I'm not here to fight tonight. I'm here for something else—something far more important.

The girls and the youngest pups.

I'm close to finding them, now. I can feel it in my gut. The wind carries the faintest whisper of their voices, muffled but unmistakable, coming from somewhere deep in the camp. I stay still, waiting, listening, my heart beating like a drum beneath my armor.

There. The sound is clearer now. A quiet sob. A soft, desperate whisper, followed by a closer scream of an older girl. My blood runs cold, but I don't move. Not yet.

I know the layout of the camp well enough to guess where the girls are being held. The shack in the far corner. It's away from the main tents, hidden behind piles of crates and barrels. I've seen it before from my position in the shrubs. The wind shifted earlier and I smelled the unmistakable smell of their fear. There are no guards near it— just a few sentries at the camp's entrance.

I exhale slowly, slipping from the shadows and making my way toward the shack. My boots are silent on the ground, my movements practiced, calculated. The only sounds are the occasional crackle of the fires and the drunken laughter of the rogues who are oblivious to my presence.

I reach the shack's back wall and crouch, peering through a crack in the wood. Through the gap, I can make out shapes inside—figures huddled together, wrapped in tattered blankets. Their faces are pale, their eyes wide with fear. They're the ones we've been searching for, the ones who've been stolen in the dead of night and left to rot here, far from their families.

I press my hand to the wood, a silent promise to them. I will get them out. I will not leave without them.

I start to pull back, my body tensing, ready to slip away unnoticed when the hairs on the back of my neck stand on end. The rotten stench of rogue combined with sweat and body funk enters my sensitive nose. I freeze. There's movement behind me. The crunch of boots on the gravel. A shout, sharp and clear. "Who's there?!"

My heart skips a beat, and before I can even react, the glow of a flashlight shines across the ground. Two guards round the corner, their eyes locking on mine.

I'm caught. I have never been caught on a surveillance mission before. It's too late to shift. The guards are too close, too quick. One lunges forward, grabbing my arm and twisting it behind my back. Pain flares through my shoulder as I struggle, but

I'm outnumbered. The other guard takes my cell phone, tossing it aside with a sneer.

"Thought you could sneak around, eh?" the first guard sneers, digging his boot into the back of my knee, forcing me to the ground.

I grunt, trying to twist free, but they're already binding my hands with silver cuffs, the metal burning my skin. The second guard grabs a two by four and before I can duck, hits me in the middle of my back; I can feel the vertebrae shatter. My wolf, Pine, tries to heal it, but the silver prevents him from doing much. A third guard appears, dragging me to my feet pulling me to some unknown destination. I don't resist. I can't. The silver is weakening me by the second. The girls are still inside, but now, I'm the one being dragged away.

As a last-ditch effort, I use my strongest link, the mate link with David to try to call for help. David may be an omega, but he can at least let Alpha know I've been captured. I just hope I'm not too far from the pack for it to work.

"Take him to the Master," the first guard barks, his voice heavy with disdain.

I'm shoved toward the heart of the camp, my mind racing. There's a knot of panic in my chest, but I suppress it. I can't afford to lose focus, despite the pain and weakness from the silver. Not now. Not when I've come so close.

I glance back over my shoulder, my eyes catching the faint glow from the shack. The girls are still there, still alive, still waiting.

I'll find a way out. Whether by myself or being rescued by my pack, I'll find a way. My last thoughts as I fade to darkness are that when I heal, I'll burn this camp to the ground, these guards, the Master, and that human, too.

Chapter Sixteen
Raining Blood

Beta Jackson

The tight slickness of my mate's pussy slides down my cock. The kids are asleep, patrols have checked in with all clear and all seems quiet on the pack lands tonight. All but my mate's sweet moans as she slowly rides my dick. Her perfect breasts gently bounce in rhythm. Just the sight of her has me on the edge of exploding. I reach my hand between her folds to rub her clit, wanting to climax with her. I am teetering on the edge of exploding.

"Beta, Beta!" a frantic voice yells, accompanying the pounding at my front door. Melissa sinks down, completely sheathing my cock in her puss, causing me to explode inside her. She leans down to kiss me as I cum, pulling away and sliding off me.

"Mon chére" I reach out to her as she slides off me. She wraps a sheet around herself as she gets out of bed.

"Just a minute." She yells at whoever is at the door. "Duty calls, Love." She chuckles as she tosses me some shorts and heads to the shower. Fuck, she didn't get to cum.

Tugging on my shorts, I stumble to the front door, praying to the Moon Goddess that this commotion doesn't wake the kids. The prayer is barely out of my mouth when a sharp cry pierces the quiet from Lizzy's room, followed by the soft patter of tiny feet racing down the hall. Lars must be heading to comfort her. Not tonight. Please, not tonight. I was hoping for one night surrounded by peace and goodness in this world, but I believe evil is approaching.

As I swing the door open, the sight before me sends a chill down my spine. Omega David, John's mate, stands trembling on my doormat. His eyes are wild, red-rimmed, and filled with something close to panic. Omegas are rarely frantic—it's not in their nature. That fact alone slams me into business mode like a punch to the gut.

"What's wrong?" My voice comes out sharper than I intend, but it has the desired effect. David stumbles over the threshold, clutching the doorframe like it's the only thing keeping him upright. His breathing is erratic, shallow gasps that sound almost painful.

I guide him into the living room, my hand firm on his arm. He moves awkwardly, as if injured, every step a strain. His face twists in pain as he lowers himself onto the couch.

"David, did you hurt your back?" I ask, crouching in front of him.

He shakes his head vehemently, the motion jerky and desperate. "No. It's not me; it's John," he chokes out between gasps. "Something's wrong with John."

The words hit like a blow to the chest, but I push down the rising dread. I can't afford to lose my head right now. I squeeze his shoulder and speak firmly. "Breathe, David. Ya gotsta tell me what happened."

He nods, his breathing ragged but starting to even out. "I felt it," he whispers, his voice trembling. "Through the bond. John: he's hurt. I got a weak link from him... it was so faint. All I could make out was 'love you.' He tried to say more, but" David's voice cracks, and his body shakes with suppressed sobs. "Then I felt something hit my back. It wasn't mine; it was his pain. I *know* it."

My jaw tightens, and my stomach churns. Feeling one's mate's injury through the bond is rare, but when it happens, the physical and emotional echoes can cripple the surviving mate.

"Explain," I order, sharper this time. The word lashes out, cold and commanding. Normally, I'd never issue an order to an omega; it's cruel to force their submissive instincts, but time is against us, and David can't afford the luxury of breaking down right now.

His body stiffens at the compulsion, and his eyes dart to mine, pleading. "I... I don't know everything. Just the link. It was weak, like he was barely holding on. And then... then the pain. It felt like something broke his back."

He breaks, his sobs echoing through the room. I look up to see Melissa standing in the doorway, her face etched with worry. "Lars took Lizzy to his room. The kids are fine," she assures me, stepping into the room and kneeling beside David. Her hand moves in slow, soothing circles on his back.

"It'll be okay," she says gently. "The warriors will find him."

I stand and force my voice to steady. "David, we know where he was. The Alpha already has the location of the camp from when his unit came back this afternoon. We'll find him." I lean closer, meeting his tear-streaked face with unwavering determination. "I swear it on the Moon. We'll bring him home."

What I don't say aloud weighs heavy in my chest. I didn't swear to bring John home alive. That promise, as much as I want to make it, might not be mine to give. But I'll be damned if I leave my friend, my packmate, in the hands of evil like Piers Jameson—not alive, not dead, not ever.

By the time I reach the war room, our top warriors are already assembled. Alpha Leonard stands by the map table, his arms crossed and his expression grim. Beside him, Sara, our Luna, is sharpening his blade with a slow, deliberate rhythm, readying it for him to go to battle. Not that he needs a sword, he's a weapon naturally. Their eyes snap to me as I enter.

"Is the team ready?" I ask, my voice cutting through the tension.

"Yes," Alpha replies. "The camp is in a clearing near the western ridge, about 10 miles past our border. It's fortified, but their numbers are smaller than ours. With a precision strike, we can take them out before they realize what hit them."

"Good." I step closer, studying the map. The enemy's camp is marked in red, nestled in a valley surrounded by dense forest. Perfect for a surprise assault. "Lars ran this, being chased by rogues, carrying a baby in his mouth? That boy is stronger than we thought, Len."

"Yeah, don't forget, it's your job to teach him to control all that strength and power. And his mouth, if you can. Boy curses far too much for a three-year-old." Nodding in response, I think about the task at hand. I don't enjoy taking lives, but tonight will be cleansing the world of some of the evil we battle against. Piers Jameson, his witch Baleen, and their team have committed some of the evilest acts thinkable. Rape, murder, murder of newborns, kidnapping... none of that can be allowed in this world, and I am certainly not going to allow it near my pack.

Orion paces in my head, eager to get on with the battle. His mission is to destroy the evil that hurt our pups. We've already taken out Baleen, now it's time to destroy anyone else who had a hand in this evil.

"Divide into two units," I instruct the room. "Alpha, you'll lead the flanking team. Circle around and hit them from the south. Gamma team, you're with me. We'll take the north side and push inward. Speed and stealth are our priorities. No rogue leaves that camp alive."

Lenny nods, his green eyes flashing with determination. "Understood." When it comes to battle, I'm in charge. Len needs to focus on what he does best, tearing apart our enemy bit by bit.

Minutes later, we're moving through the forest, the night cloaking us like a shadow. My warriors are silent, even in wolf form, their movements precise and practiced. We must look a sight, wolves moving through the forest in formation, some with human weapons strapped to them. I lead the northern team, every sense honed and alert. The faint scent of smoke reaches me first, carried on the breeze. Then, I hear it, the low murmur of voices, the crackle of a fire.

We're close.

I signal to the group to halt and crouch low. From here, I can see the outlines of the camp: a handful of crude tents, a central fire pit, and several figures milling about. Rogues. Their postures are relaxed, complacent. They are all in human form, but their stench permeates the forest. *Excellent,* Orion links me, *Human form is squishy and easy to kill.* They have no idea we're here.

I raise my hand, and Archer shifts and readies his bow. The first arrow flies, silent and deadly. It strikes true, dropping a rogue before they can even gasp. The camp erupts in chaos, and that's when we strike.

We move as one, a lethal force tearing through the night. I shift mid-leap, Orion exploding from within me. My claws tear through the throat of the first rogue I encounter, his scream cut short as I dispatch him swiftly. Around me, my warriors do the same: shifting, striking, eliminating. The aptly named Archer stands on the raised berm we approached from and sends arrow after arrow into the rogues.

Alpha's wolf, Blizzard seems to be having fun. A white streak tearing through the camp, ripping the throats and guts out of wolf after wolf, his fur reddening more with each kill. Len has been my best friend since we were kids, and I fought with him many times. But it never ceases to amaze me the speed that wolf can kill with.

The rogues scramble to defend themselves, but they're unorganized and panicked. Half don't even try to shift. One lunges at me, his blade catching the moonlight. Orion hops to the side, turns and leaps at him, driving him into the dirt, our jaws closing around his throat. Unlike many wolves, Orion and I are able to share control of our body, we work together so well. Clamping down, but not yet hard enough to kill, we give the young rogue a chance to submit to us. He swipes at our belly, and Orion crushes his throat, pulling out his trachea and swallowing it whole before letting out a roar like howl, Redwood Pack's battle cry.

Did you have to eat it? I ask my wolf.

Tasty. Is all he replies before pouncing on a rogue in human form that is about to flank Archer. Quicker than Archer can launch another arrow, Orion tears out the spine of the rogue and tosses it aside. *Human not tasty, give gas. Orion chirps* as he turns to take down yet another rogue.

Out of the corner of my eye, I see Alpha Lenny take down two more rogues with his claws, moving with a precision that reminds me why he's the Alpha. Behind the chaos, the gamma's team emerges from the southern flank, trapping the remaining enemies in a deadly circle. It takes only seconds for the highly trained wolves to gut each remaining rogue.

The battle is over in minutes. When the last rogue falls, the forest goes still, the silence broken only by the ragged breaths of my warriors.

I shift back to human form, my chest heaving as I survey the carnage. There are bodies everywhere, yet none are packmates. The fire in the center of the camp sputters weakly, casting flickering shadows over the bodies strewn across the ground.

Alpha drags a fighting shifter, in human form, out of a tent. It's Piers. We have him. He's dressed in an immaculate suit, having let his men die instead of fighting with them. Far too dressy for a man, if one could call this level of evil a man, living in the woods. Making quick eye contact, I know what Lenny wants to do. A quick mind-link *"end him"* is all it takes for my Alpha to take one clawed hand and rip Piers Jameson's disgusting head off.

As I look at Piers' head Lenny holds up for me, the veins and ligaments dripping with fluids, his eyes stuck open in shock for eternity, I let out a sigh of relief. No more sisters will be kidnapped or killed by this evil rogue. No more pups killed or experimented on. Evil, at least this manifestation of it, has been stopped tonight.

"Secure the area," I order. "Search the tents. I want to know everything. Search for the pups and girls and Gamma John. Find the young boy Arioch, he's about five with dirty blonde hair, keep him separate from the rest of the kids you find." I link the warriors the image of Arioch Lars shared with Alpha Lenny and I when we were questioning him. "Look for any evidence of where the boys' camp and the younger girls are. Alpha and I will search Jameson's tent."

As my warriors spread out to carry out my orders, I take a moment to breathe. These rogues made a fatal mistake joining Jameson. Redwood Pack is strong, united, and ruthless when it needs to be. And anyone who threatens our safety—or the safety of the innocent—will meet the same fate.

Jameson's tent was a scene of horror. Two young girls' bodies were found on the bed. Both were dead and had been for days. Bite marks on their necks looked like someone had attempted to mark them, though the teeth marks were too small to be an adult. Documenting the scene as evidence for the Council, we collected what we could.

"Do you think Arioch bit them?" I asked Lenny as we carefully moved the girls' bodies outside to where our troops were placing bodies of other girls found dead. We'd start a pyre and send their souls to the Moon Goddess before we left. A small team of our men were already collecting the wood for the pyre.

The dead rogues would be buried in a mass grave to prevent humans from finding the bodies. The worms would feast for months on them, and their evil souls would be forced to what the humans called

Hell. Never again would their souls walk the Earth.

Hoping some good would come from the horrific scene, I returned to Jameson's tent, hoping to find anything that would lead us to the camp the young boys were being held in, or where the younger girls were being kept. I found tons of documents on the results of the "experiments" done by Baleen, maps of the locations of every Pack in California and Nevada, and battle plans. He'd planned to attack or had attacked every pack in the area. There was also a strange book, which smelled strongly of sulfur, with a strange cross-like symbol with a horizontal infinity symbol at the bottom. I collected everything for the Council. Except the book. My instincts tell me not to let that book fall into the hands of the Council. They would be tempted to increase their power with the knowledge in the mysterious smelly book. So, that book goes in my safe. Unopened.

Chapter Seventeen
Some Kind of Monster

Alpha Leonard

One hundred and three. One hundred and three pups who never got the chance to live. That's the grim tally we uncovered in a burn pit at the back of the camp. The skulls—so small, so fragile—weren't even fully fused. To count them, we had to rely on the maxillae scattered through the ash and dirt. The sight alone would crush even the strongest of hearts, and once again, I see my warriors break down, tears streaming down faces that have weathered countless battles.

This is the weight we carry from this victory in this battle against evil.

But the horrors don't stop there. We found the girls, the older sisters and cousins of the boys we'd managed to rescue during the attack on our pack. Too late. Too damn late to save their innocence. Girls as young as thirteen, brutalized by rogues who used them for their twisted pleasures and as tools for Jameson's depraved experiments with that witch. I feel my claws digging into my palms as I think of the agony they've endured.

I won't let them walk back to our pack lands, not after everything they've been through. I call for the buses, making sure the girls can travel in safety and some semblance of comfort. Once we're back, we'll begin the delicate work of reuniting them with their families. First, though, they need to feel safe. They need to know that this nightmare is over.

Jackson's interrogation of the witch revealed another complication. They had a human working with them—a loose end we couldn't find at the camp. And then there's Arioch, Jameson's son. A child, yes, but corrupted beyond his years. From what Lars recounted, Arioch is as cruel as his father, though how much of that is nurture and how much is nature, I can't say. Executing a child isn't an option, but he will be a problem when we find him. The Council will have to figure out a way to rehabilitate him, if that's even possible. The bite marks on those girls' necks are too small to belong to anyone else. The thought churns my stomach.

A sudden cry snaps me from my thoughts. "Healer! We need a healer over here!"

I sprint toward the sound, my heart pounding as I weave through the camp. The source of the commotion becomes clear when I reach a small, rusted metal shed, its door wrenched open by Archer's claws. Inside, my gamma, John, lies crumpled on the floor. My stomach sinks.

Silver cuffs bite into his wrists, preventing his natural healing. His body is twisted in a horrifying way, his spine clearly broken. Cuts, bruises, and a mix of blood and dirt cover him, while one leg and the opposite arm are shattered. The metallic tang of wolfsbane fills the air.

The healers rush in with a backboard, their faces pale but determined. Silver can kill shifters with enough exposure, and John's already endured too much. Extending one claw, I break the locks on the cuffs and toss them far from the shed, my own skin burning slightly from the brief contact.

Jackson appears at my side, his nose wrinkling. "Wolfsbane," he mutters. "That smell ... after Lars, I'll never forget it."

"He's alive," one of the healers announces, her voice steady but urgent. "Alpha, we need to get him to Doctor Hill immediately. His injuries are severe, and he might not have the strength to heal his back on his own."

I nod, my mind racing. "Take him on the last bus. Ensure he's stabilized and safe."

We've collected all the evidence we could find, packed it onto the buses, and secured the girls. The remaining warriors, including myself, will run back as is our tradition after battle. But first, we'll burn this cursed place to the ground.

Everything we've seen here shows just how evil Piers Jameson was. He was a monster, raising a monster, working with monsters. And not the type of monsters the humans think we wolf shifters, werewolves they call us, are. These monsters were the true ones, evil incarnate.

Standing at the edge of the camp, I watch as the flames rise, consuming the horrors and the memories of this nightmare. The humans will think this was started by a lightning strike. The fire is cleansing, but it doesn't erase what we've seen, or the scars left behind. We'll carry those with us, just as we always do.

Chapter Eighteen
Heaven and Hell

Beta Jackson

One hundred and three. I can't stop repeating that number in my mind. One hundred and three little lives snuffed out before they even had the chance to begin. One hundred and three futures stolen; mates who would never meet their other halves, mothers who would never hear the laughter of their pups, dreams extinguished before they could take shape. And Elizabeth, my little Lizzy, so easily could have been one of them.

The thought twists in my chest like a knife. If not for the courage of a handful of women in the camp, and Lars, my little shifter, I might not have either of my pups. I shudder to think how close I came to never having them. The thought of it is raw, like an open wound I can't bear to touch yet can't ignore.

Now, as we load the girls and the few surviving women onto the buses bound for the Pack, I force myself to stay focused. There's work to do, and I can't afford to let my emotions get the better of me, not here, not now. The air is heavy with a mix of relief and grief, the survivors clutching each other as though letting go might break them.

When the last of them is safely aboard, we turn our attention to the camp. It's eerily silent now, its dark history seared into every shadowed corner. We clear it of anything that might alert the humans to the camp's existence, or worse the existence of wolf shifters or the supernatural world. We wipe away every trace of what happened here, even as the memories linger, etched into our minds.

And then we burn it.

The flames roar to life, devouring the twisted remnants of a place that should never have existed. The funeral pyre burns at the edge of the forest. The burn zone a warning to evil, a symbol of destruction but also of rebirth of the forest from the evil that tainted it. The fire lights the night sky, and I stand for a moment, watching the smoke curl upward as though carrying the souls of those lost to a place far better than this.

Finally, when there's nothing left but ash and embers, we do what tradition demands. We run. It's a somber victory, this run, the kind that reminds us of what we've won but also of what it cost. The wind tears at my face as my feet pound the earth, the steady rhythm a grounding force against the storm inside me. Around me, the others run too, their howls piercing the night, a collective cry of both triumph and mourning. We run not just for ourselves but for those who can no longer run, those who never got the chance to run, for the one hundred and three who will never know this freedom.

And as the Pack's borders come into view, the first rays of dawn breaking over the horizon, I hold tight to the hope that, somehow, we can make all this mean something.

After a quick shower and a change of clothes, I find myself standing in Lizzy's room, cradling her in my arms. Her tiny hand clutches the fabric of my shirt as if she never wants to let go. It hasn't even been a month since she came into my life, yet she's already claimed the title of *Pa's Little Girl*. And Lars, mischievous, dirt-loving Lars, is undeniably *Pa's Boy*.

I can't help but marvel at how everything seems to have fallen into place. Is this real? Pups, a mate, a family; it feels like a dream. Just weeks ago, darkness loomed over my life. I was a 23-year-old unmated shifter, running out of time before my wolf would start to go mad, grieving my twin and angry all the time. The darkness threatening to take away everything before it had a chance to bloom. Now, I'm surrounded by light, and the thought of losing it fills me with a fierce protectiveness.

Alpha called a meeting of the ranked Pack members for noon to review the evidence we gathered. That gives me just enough time for an early lunch with my pups before I drop them back off at daycare for the meeting. Or at least, that was the plan.

Lars, true to form, is in his room, changing out of an outfit that's somehow covered in dirt despite spending less than thirty minutes at daycare. How does he manage it? From the moment Mel dropped them off to when I picked them up, he turned his pristine clothes into a canvas of smudges and stains. I chuckle as I hear him humming to himself while trying to wrestle on a fresh shirt.

I thought about leaving the kids to eat with their classmates, but Lizzy is still too young to notice the difference. Besides, Len already picked up his boys, so Lars' best friends weren't there to share lunch either. With that in mind, I head to the small kitchen in my apartment to make Lars his favorite, ravioli. The smell of tomato and cheese soon fills the air, drawing Lars out of his room like a magnet.

We eat together, Lars enthusiastically talking about his day between bites, while Lizzy babbles happily in her car seat. It's a simple moment, but one I'll treasure. Afterward, I help Lars clean up, again, before gathering both pups on the couch for a cuddle. Lizzy nestles into my chest, her warmth a soothing balm, while Lars leans against my side, his hand gripping mine. I hold onto the moment as long as I can, knowing the responsibilities waiting for me.

When the clock ticks closer to noon, I gently place Lizzy in her stroller and take Lars by the hand. I can't bring myself to drop them back at daycare; not after what we saw at Jameson's camp. The memory still sends a chill down my spine. I need my pups near me, where I can protect them.

The conference room is across from Len's office, and as I approach, I notice I'm not the only one who feels this way. Sara and Len are already there, their children with them. Len holds newborn Paisley as if she's the most fragile treasure in the world, the same way I held Lizzy before lunch. It's comforting to see that same instinct mirrored in my Alpha.

Delta Jenny appears, her calm efficiency shining through. She gently takes Paisley and Lizzy, cradling Paisley in one arm, pushing Lizzy in the stroller while ushering the boys across the hall to the playroom attached to Len's office. The sight of my pups being cared for by someone I trust eases the tension in my chest, but only slightly.

As the door closes behind her, I take a deep breath and turn my attention to the room. The weight of the meeting ahead settles on my shoulders, but I remind myself of what I'm fighting for: Lizzy's smile when she farts, Lars' mischievous grin, the family I never thought I'd have, and the chance for the lost and kidnapped pups to return to their families.

Chapter Nineteen
Green Hell

Meetings are the most boring thing humans ever do. If they weren't packmates, I'd eat half these people, all the talking over each other and bickering. Just listen to Alpha and take turns talking! It's not that hard.

Alpha is going over the maps found at Jameson's camp. I watch the humans, their gestures, their expressions, as they talk over one another. But I'm not just watching. I'm listening, my ears swiveling toward every voice, picking up the undercurrents of tension and excitement. Then, something clicks in my head. The witch's chant starts playing like an old melody:

> Between Alfred's Church where crows attack and George's former dark side ranch. From salty seas to

where false evil turns to breeze. That's where you'll find the pups with fleas.

Jackson, my human, likes to watch all sorts of movies. Once, he watched an old black-and-white film where birds attacked people in a coastal village. I remember him saying the actual village is near here.

Boss, where's that bird movie village? Wasn't that movie made by a guy named Alfred? I ask Jackson, curious if my instincts are right. I'm just a wolf, after all. Sometimes human things blur together for me.

Jackson blinks, his hand pausing mid-air over the map. "Oh, Goddess, you're right," he mutters, his voice tinged with excitement. "What was the whole poem?"

I repeat the chant to him, every word etched into my memory. His eyes light up, and I feel a flicker of pride.

"Alpha, I think I figured it out," Jackson says, loud enough to capture the room's attention. I growl low, just enough for him to hear. Taking credit for my observation, are we?

"Well, Orion noticed it," he amends, smirking at me through our shared mind. That's better. Alpha nods for him to continue, his sharp gaze fixed on Jackson.

Jackson recites the chant; his finger tracing lines on the map. He points to a little coastal village. "This has to be Alfred's Church. The Birds, the old movie, it fits." His finger slides to another location. "And this spot is the 'dark side ranch' of George."

He hesitates, frowning as he tries to decipher the last line. "But I'm not sure about 'salty seas' or 'false evil turns to breeze.'"

Alpha steps forward, his imposing presence silencing the room as he marks the map where Jackson pointed. Before anyone can speak, Luna gasps, the sound sharp and clear in the quiet.

"Salty seas and evil turns to breeze!" she exclaims, snatching the pen from Alpha. Her energy crackles through the air as she marks a dot on a peninsula labeled with a prison. "This prison holds the human death row. 'Evil turns to breeze'; it's where executions are supposed to happen."

The room hums with understanding. She grabs a ruler and connects the dots Alpha and she marked, forming a narrow triangle. The lines seem to pulse with significance, a beacon of direction.

"This is where we'll find the pups," Alpha declares, his voice resolute.

My tail swishes once, a surge of determination coursing through me. But then reality sets in: human territory. That means no wolf form. Humans get twitchy when wolves roam where they're not supposed to.

I huff, glancing at Jackson. *Guess we doing this your way, Boss.*

Beta Jackson

My way, my wolf says. Apparently, "my way" involves driving around in a cramped puke green Toyota Prius that is too dang tiny for my large frame, windows rolled down, trying to sniff out shifters hidden among humans. The scent of leather and stale fast food permeates the car, a far cry from the fresh air of the woods. Despite

Orion's bellyaching, this is the best method we have to stay under the radar.

The faint trace of rogue shifters leads me to a nearby nature preserve. Parking the car, with no small amount of relief to get out of the claustrophobic clutches of the miniature car, I stretch, letting Orion, my wolf, take the lead.

Two rogues, Boss, he informs me, his voice low and bristling with tension. *And a faint smell of girl pup.*

I can't afford to get my hopes up. The scent might just belong to a family of rogues passing through. But there's also a chance it's part of Jameson's group, and more importantly, the camp where the missing male pups are being held. The boys we rescued after the attack on our pack said the girls had been with them at the training camp before being separated. If they're here, I might have stumbled onto what we've been searching for.

Grumbling under my breath, I slam the car door shut. Why Lenny insisted I leave my truck behind is beyond me. Something about being "less conspicuous." As if this tin can of a car doesn't scream "out of place" when parked near the woods. I push the irritation aside and get my head back in the game.

Orion's nose leads us deeper into the preserve, past trails that are well-trodden by hikers and into terrain humans rarely venture. The faint scent strengthens, guiding us to a hidden camp nestled in a dense thicket. It's well-concealed, nearly impossible for a human to stumble upon by accident.

What I see there stops me cold. It's another version of Hell on Earth, built by Jameson and his evil cronies. Young boys, barely out of infancy, are being forced to train as warriors. Their movements are stiff, fear etched into every line of their faces. Rogues bark orders at them, striking out when the boys falter. The sharp crack of a slap against skin makes Orion growl, a sound low and dangerous in my chest. It takes every ounce of restraint I have to keep from letting him take over and tearing these evil couillon apart.

Not as evil as Jameson and his witch, maybe. But anyone who beats pups for any reason is a monster in my book.

The scent of the girl pup is fainter here, mingled with the sweat and fear of the boys. She might have been moved recently, or... I don't let myself dwell on the darker possibilities. One crisis at a time.

I make careful notes of the camp's coordinates, memorizing landmarks in case I lose signal. I can't act alone, not without backup. Silently, I retreat the way I came, my heart heavy but my resolve steely. Back at the car, I shoot a text to Lenny at the war room, including the location and everything I've seen.

"Found them," I type, my fingers trembling with fury and determination, making me miss letters on the small keyboard. "Send reinforcements."

Sliding back into the driver's seat of the cursed Prius, I grip the wheel tightly, forcing myself to breathe. We're close to ending this now. Closer than we've ever been. And when the time comes, we'll make these rogues pay for what they've done. Mark my words.

Chapter Twenty
Invisible Kid

Lars

It's been forebber since I was in my wolf form. Ever since the bad wolves attacked us in da safe room. Ma is busy washing Izzy, so I take off my itchy shorts and teeshirt and shift into Thor's body. I jump up on my bed and curl up with my alligator stuffy and take a nap.

Lady Melissa

After settling Elizabeth down for her nap, I quietly close her door and tiptoe down the hall. My thoughts are still swirling with her soft, sleepy murmurs when I push open Lars' door. But instead of finding my little boy, I freeze.

There, curled up on his bed, is my wolf pup. Thor. His dark blue wolflit eyes gleam up at me, catching the light filtering through the curtains. His sleek fur bristles slightly, and his little tail thumps against the mattress in greeting.

"Hello, Thor," I say softly, sitting down on the edge of the bed. My hand instinctively reaches out to stroke his head, my fingers threading through the silken fur as I scratch behind his ears. He leans into the touch with a small, contented whine. No matter how wild and ancient his soul might be, Thor is still only three in this lifetime, a child trying to navigate his dual nature.

"How's my adorable pup doing?" I ask, my voice warm but laced with concern.

Thor's ears twitch, and he looks up at me with a somber expression that doesn't match his playful form. "We miss running in the woods, Ma," he says, his voice soft and plaintive. "Alpha said we can only shift when it's just family or in emergencies. That means we can't run in the woods in wolf body. We can't go see the moon."

His words hit me like a stone, and I pause mid-stroke, my heart aching for him. How could I have missed this? In our attempts to keep Lars, and Thor, safe, we've unknowingly denied him something fundamental to his being.

"Oh, sweetheart," I murmur, pulling him into a gentle hug. His furry head rests against my chest, and I can feel the steady rhythm of his breathing.

The truth is, none of us, me, Jackson, or even Alpha Lenny, stopped to think about what it means for a shifter to be separated from the moon's pull for so long. Shifters draw their strength, their vitality, from the Moon Goddess, and being under her light is more than tradition, it's nourishment for the soul.

"I'll talk to Pa when he gets home," I promise, my voice resolute. "We'll figure out a way for you to run, Thor. To feel the moonlight again. I won't let you be without it any longer."

Thor looks up at me, his dark blue eyes shimmering with hope, and his tail wags again, this time with a little more energy.

But even as I hold him close, guilt gnaws at me. In the chaos of war against the master, the whirlwind of starting a new family, and adjusting to our new roles as parents, I overlooked something so essential. Thor has gone from surviving on his own to being cared for, and yet none of us considered his primal needs.

As soon as Jackson gets home from his mission, this will be fixed by a little family moon run.

Chapter Twenty-One
And Justice For All

Alpha Leonard

Gamma John lies motionless on the hospital bed, his broad chest rising and falling in a slow, steady rhythm, a fragile thread connecting him to the waking world. His mate, David, is slumped in the chair beside him, head resting lightly against John's hip. David's fingers curl around John's hand, his grip firm despite the exhaustion etched into his face. The dark circles under his eyes and the slight tremble in his posture speak of sleepless nights and whispered prayers.

I glance around the infirmary, a place that's become all too familiar these days. Between my boys, Lars, Elizabeth, and now John, it feels like I've spent more time here than anywhere else lately. The sterile smell of antiseptic clings to my clothes, and the steady beeping of monitors has become a grim sort of background music. It's enough to make anyone's nerves fray, but there's no room for weakness here, not when one of my best warriors lies injured.

Doctor Hill moves quietly around the room, his expression one of practiced calm. Despite his nerves around Jackson, he's one of the best shifter doctors in the world, and he knows it. John's in a medically induced coma, his body limp, his mind tucked away somewhere safe while his wolf takes the lead. His wolf, Pine is working overtime to heal him. It's a delicate balance, though. Too much strain, and even the wolf's magic might not be enough to fix his back.

I take a step closer to the bed, my gaze falling on John's face. He looks peaceful, almost like he's just sleeping, but the pallor of his skin and the faint bruises healing along his jaw tell a different story. Seeing him like this, a pillar of strength brought down is enough to send a pang of unease through me. He's Gamma John, the one who's always there when the pack needs him. And now, we can only hope he's strong enough to claw his way back to us.

David stirs slightly in his chair, mumbling something under his breath. His hand not grasping John's brushes against John's side, as though the simple touch might be enough to tether him here. The love between mates can be calming to the soul, helping heal as well. While John has more moon magic than David, David's calming Omega magic should help keep Pine and John fighting to come back to us fully healed.

I lean against the wall, arms crossed, thinking about every thing we have to deal with now, finding the rest of the pups Jameson has hidden, hoping my gamma recovers, shortlisting wolves to replace him if he doesn't. "He's a fighter," Doctor Hill says softly, as if sensing my thoughts. His voice is steady, confident. "If anyone in this pack can make it through this, it's John, you, Beta Jackson or maybe Beta's pup Lars."

"Ha, Jax is so stubborn, I doubt anything would stop him."

"That man is... intense." The doctor's eyes widen as we discuss my best friend and beta. As we chat, I get a simple text from the man himself. *Send reinforcements.*

As I sit cramped in this wretched little car, the air thick with the scent of old fast food and cheap leather air freshener, I keep my eyes on the road ahead, waiting. Waiting for our troops to roll in, for the plan to kick off, for the chance to do what needs doing. My fingers drum against the steering wheel, the rhythm a poor disguise for the storm brewing inside me. My jaw clenches tighter with every passing second, thoughts swirling like a storm in my head.

I think about my own pups, my heart clenches so hard it feels like it might break. By the Goddess, they came so close, too damn close, to having their little lives stolen by these couillon before I even knew they existed. The memory sends a chill crawling up my spine. Evil, I've learned, doesn't just lurk in shadows; it strides boldly, stopping at nothing, tearing through lives like a hurricane. It's that thought, the raw injustice of it, that keeps me here. Keeps my hands steady despite the rage simmering just beneath the surface.

The trees stretch out beyond the windshield, their dark silhouettes standing like shadowy sentinels under a starless sky. The world is eerily quiet, save for the occasional whisper of the wind through the woodss. My eyes search the darkness, and my chest tightens with the weight of imagination, those poor little ones, frightened and alone, wondering if anyone's coming for them. "We're comin', pups," I whisper, my voice hoarse and thick with resolve. "Hold on now."

I picture them: wide-eyed, trembling, clutching at whatever scraps of hope they've managed to hold onto. I hope the rogues haven't beaten that hope out of them completely. Maybe, just maybe, some of them will see their mommas and daddies again. Maybe they'll run into familiar arms, hear soft voices telling them it's over, that they're safe now. But not all of them will. That truth hangs heavy, like a storm cloud. Some will end up in the council's foster system, shuffled from pack to pack like pawns on a chessboard. Because for too many, there's no family left to go back to. The monsters saw to that, leaving nothing but empty homes and shattered lives in their wake.

But there's still hope. There has to be. We got justice for Lars, Elizabeth, and the she wolves and pups at the other camp. And now, we're here to get justice for all the victims of Jameson's twisted group. Not every pup will have a family waiting for them, but at least they'll have their packs or new families. Arms to hold them, voices to remind them they're loved, a chance to heal. It ain't much. It ain't enough. But it's better than the nightmare they've been living.

The wind picks up, rattling the branches outside like skeletal fingers against the glass. I take a deep breath, trying to steady the fire roaring in my chest. This fight isn't just about us or even our territory. It's not on pack lands or borders, where we could move freely. We're deep in human territory, in an area where their rules and their eyes make every step a risk.

To make things worse, California doesn't have many wild wolves, barely any, really. Most of our warriors, with their wolf forms resembling the native grays, will stick out like a sore thumb.

California considers those wolves endangered. A fight here means walking a razor's edge. We'll need to strike fast and precise, minimizing losses while keeping our secret safe from prying human eyes. If they catch sight of us, it'll be trackers, tranquilizers, or worse. They'll lock us in some zoo, studying us like curiosities. The balance between the supernatural and natural world has always been fragile, and one mistake could shatter it entirely.

But none of that matters right now. What matters is the little ones. They're out there, waiting for someone to come for them, to pull them from the clutches of evil and bring them home. By Goddess, we're gonna do just that. No matter the cost, no matter the risks, we're bringing them home.

Alpha finally links me, his voice steady but tinged with urgency. Our warriors are close enough for me to issue instructions and coordinate the attack. Relief washes over me for a brief moment, but it's quickly swallowed by the weight of what's to come. Being deep in human territory makes everything harder. We have to move carefully, silently, without drawing the wrong kind of attention. A sudden influx of people, some armed, near a nature preserve could raise alarms we can't afford to deal with.

I open the mental link to the group, sending the camp's coordinates along with my orders. *Remember, we're in human territory*, I remind them, my voice sharp and clear in their minds. *This area is hard for humans to access, but it's not impossible. Wolves aren't common here, and if any of you are caught in wolf form, the humans won't hesitate to capture you. They'll track you, collar you, or worse, throw you into some exhibit in a zoo. So be stealthy. Be quick. No mistakes.*

I pause for a moment, letting my words sink in before continuing. *Your primary targets are the adult wolves in the camp. They're the ones responsible for all of this, the kidnappings, the brainwashing, the training. They've earned what's coming to them. As for the pups...* My voice falters slightly, but I steel myself. *Leave them alone unless they attack. If they do, incapacitate only. They are victims: manipulated, terrified, forced to fight for their captors. But after what I saw in this camp, after what those adults did to train them...* My breath hitches, a surge of anger breaking through my calm facade. *If you must defend yourself, don't hesitate. Do what you have to do.*

Deltas, after we secure the camp, you'll enter to calm and collect the pups to bring them back to our territory to begin getting everyone home.

I feel the warriors' resolve through the link, their affirmations like distant echoes in my mind. Not one of them objects. Good. They understand the stakes.

I survey the area from my cramped position in the car, my eyes scanning the dense trees and shadowed undergrowth. The camp lies just ahead, shrouded in darkness, its inhabitants unaware of what's closing in. I signal for the warriors to move into position. Their presence is a silent ripple across the mental link, each of them creeping closer, blending seamlessly with the forest's shadows.

I get to a position outside the pack, crouched in the tall bushes. Hearing a faint breathing I'd never pick up without my enhanced Beta senses, I look up in the tree above me. His dark skin camoflaguing him in the shadows, I barely make out the outline of Archer, prepped and ready with his bow and arrows.

The tension is palpable, a coiled spring ready to snap. The air is thick with anticipation, every sound amplified in the stillness, the distant rustle of leaves, the soft crunch of boots on damp earth. I can feel my pulse in my throat, a steady drumbeat that matches the countdown in my head.

Hold your positions, I whisper through the link, though I know they're already there, waiting, watching. *Wait for my signal.*

This is the moment we've prepared for, the culmination of months of searching and planning. The lives of the stolen pups, and the safety of countless others, depend on us tonight. The rogues don't know it yet, but their reign of terror ends here. Their bosses are already dead, now to take out the last remaining loyalists to the Master.

Kind of like the Battle of Nawlins, Boss. Orion chirps, reminding me of his love for history. I take a deep breath, steadying myself as I reach for the final command. This battle is about more than revenge. It's about justice. It's about protecting the vulnerable and ensuring no more pups are forced into this nightmare.

Attack, I order, my voice slicing through the mind-link like a blade. The forest comes alive with motion, shadows springing into action. The battle has begun.

Three sharp, high-pitched whistles pierce the still night air, shattering the fragile silence like shards of glass. The sound is unmistakable, a signal of death approaching. Overhead, Archer draws his bow with practiced precision, releasing three arrows in rapid succession. Each finds its mark, the faint whistle of their flight ending in the wet, sickening thud of impact.

The last rogue at the fire pit stands right before the arrow hits him, causing the arrow to land in the back just below his rib cage. The momentum drives him forward, his scream cutting the night as he collapses into the roaring flames. The fire flares to life, engulfing him, his cries a grisly beacon that summons the others.

The camp erupts in chaos. Canvas tents ripple as rogue wolves pour out, their snarls and shouts clashing with the crackling fire. My warriors spring into action, a blur of muscle and fury, meeting the rogues head-on. Blood pools glint in the firelight, fangs flash, and claws tear into flesh with merciless efficiency.

These rogues fight with the same wild disorganization as Jameson's pack at the other camp: brute force without discipline. It's their undoing. My warriors, trained for moments like this, slice through them like a well-honed blade. Blood sprays the air as throats are torn open, bellies are ripped apart, and spines are shattered in savage, final motions.

The ground soon glistens red in the firelight, littered with the broken bodies of our enemies. Only four rogues remain in the open, their snarls faltering as they realize the slaughter unfolding around them. My warriors don't pause, their relentless precision driving the rogues back with every strike.

Behind them, others sweep through the shadows, methodically searching the tents and lean-tos. Their task is critical: to find the pups we've come to rescue and to ensure no rogue escapes to tell the tale of what happened here tonight.

The camp is alive with chaos, but the tide has turned, and it seems clear: the rogues stand no chance against us. Victory seems assured when a sudden, piercing cry shatters the moment. A pup.

A rogue emerges from one of the tents, a silver blade held to the neck of a small, black hair pup, blue eyes wide as tears fill them. I freeze, seeing Lars in the rogue's arms. A growl to my right tells me Alpha is just as angry as I am.

"Everyone freeze or the pup dies." A sharp inhale and my mind restarts. It's not Lars, Lars is at home with Mel and Lizzy. But it's still one of the pups we're here to save. My mind races strategies forming and falling apart in rapid succession. The rogue shifts his grip, holding the pup like a shield. His knife gleams with lethal intent, but behind him, I catch the faint movement of our deltas, silently coaxing the other pups out of the tent.

Having been fighting in human form, with just my claws, I half shift, taking on the form humans associate with werewolves, half wolf, half man. It's our deadliest form, giving us the strength of both man and wolf, the power of the wolf with the intelligence of the man, the ability to use weapons or claws as needed.

The rogue's attention locks on me, just as I hoped. I wait until the deltas get all the pups from the tent and signal me they are clear. *In position, Beta,* Archer's voice comes over the link, calm and measured.

We've rehearsed this move countless times, a dance of timing and precision. I take another step forward, claws on my feet scraping the dirt. Shifting to a defensive position, the rogue moves the silver knife from the pup's throat and points it at me. The rogue lunges, but it's too late. Archer's arrow whistles through the air, striking true, piercing the rogue's ear canal, and ending his life in an instant. Simultaneously, I dart forward, slashing his femurs as I scoop the pup from his grasp. I roll out of reach of the rogue, already dead though his limbs flail and lash out as if his mind hasn't caught up to the brain damage and exsanguination from his femoral arteries.

The victory is short-lived. A second wave of rogues emerge from the tents as I protect the pup. Running through the camp toward our deltas, I hold the pup against me with one arm and claw out the esophagus of any enemy that gets too close.

At the camp's edge, I hand the pup to the head delta, their grip steady despite the chaos. Turning back, I leap into the fray, claws raking across a rogue's face as I rejoin the fight.

The battlefield is a blood-soaked tableau of carnage. Only one rogue remains, circling Alpha Len, who wields his sword with deliberate cruelty. Len's movements are calculated, his strikes designed to prolong the rogue's suffering. When the rogue lashes out in desperation, Len sidesteps with ease, his expression bored. Alpha always did like to play with his prey, especially when he is angry.

Len tilts his head in a wolfish manner, he's done playing. A quick strike with the sword sends the rogue's head bouncing along the ground, bouncing into the still burning fire pit.

The battle is over. Our warriors fan out, methodically clearing the camp to ensure no threats remain. We haven't found Arioch or the human accomplice, but for now, it doesn't matter. We've succeeded. The pups are safe, and Jameson's reign of terror is no more.

We've destroyed the evil known as Piers Jameson, his witch Sandia and the rogue army they built. We defeated evil and can now bring good to our species by returning these pups to where they belong.

As we regroup at the parking lot, I convince one of the smaller deltas to drive the wretched little car I came in. I settle into the bus, its larger seats a welcome reprieve after the chaos of the night. For the first time in hours, I let myself breathe. We've won, and our species will be safer for it.

Chapter Twenty-Two
We Will Rise

Beta Jackson

The pups huddle together, their wide, frightened eyes darting around the unfamiliar surroundings. Their hair is matted, their small bodies trembling with exhaustion and fear. I can feel their terror as if it were my own. My heart aches for them. Most of them are injured, with cuts, bruises, or worse. All of them carry scars I can't see, the kind that dig deep into the soul. These pups need more than just medical care; they need a lifeline, a reason to trust again.

At first, they flinch whenever I approach, their instincts screaming that I'm just another rogue, another captor ready to drag them to yet another desolate camp. Their mistrust is palpable, and I don't blame them. I tread carefully, speaking softly, my hands open and empty to show them I mean no harm. Slowly, we reunite the siblings and cousins who had been torn from their families and scattered across rogue territories. The moment they recognize one another, their wary eyes brighten, and the first slivers of hope begin to pierce through the shadows that shroud them.

I work alongside my packmates, coaxing the pups to speak, to trust us enough to share their stories. Bit by bit, their whispered words reveal the names of their packs. Some are barely audible, as though they're afraid the sound will summon their tormentors back. But we listen, we listen like their lives depend on it. Because, in a way, it does. They'll heal mentally and physically faster in their own packs, with family and pack members to guide them than they will a strange environment. Alpha doesn't waste a moment. The second we have a name, he's reaching out to the Alphas of those packs, setting the wheels in motion to bring these lost children back home.

The pups from lone wolf families are a different challenge altogether. For them, there is no pack to contact, no Alpha to call. Their stories are fragmented, memories blurred by trauma. "Do you remember anything about the night you were taken?" I ask one small girl, her voice barely above a whisper as she describes a dark forest and the smell of smoke. It's not much to go on, but it's all we have.

The weight of uncertainty is crushing. Are their families even alive? If they are, where could they be? Every clue feels like a breadcrumb in an endless forest, but we refuse to give up. I can't give up. These pups deserve more than survival; they deserve to run free, to feel the warmth of their families again. Until that day comes, we'll be their pack, their shelter, and their strength.

As the days go by, their walls begin to crumble. The pups start playing with one another, their laughter tentative at first, then spilling out like a dam breaking. It's a sound that fills me with hope. They're healing, slowly but surely. And as I watch them, I realize they're not the only ones changing. Their resilience, their ability to find light in the darkest of times, is teaching me something too. Light can come out of this darkness. Just as Lars and Lizzy found hope and family, we will find these pups' families or build them new ones.

We may not have all the answers yet, but we'll keep searching. We'll find their families, no matter how long it takes. Until then, they're home with us.

Finally, I'm back with my family after a grueling day. My muscles ache, and my mind feels like it's been pulled in a thousand directions. Between running border patrol, piecing together missing pups' families, and helping Lenny with endless paperwork, I'm drained. Exhaustion clings to me like a heavy fog as I quietly enter the apartment, already preparing myself to collapse into bed without disturbing Melissa or the kids. These long days are relentless, stealing hours I'd much rather spend with them. By the time Alpha and I finish pack business and wrap up the tedious bureaucracy of tracking down the pups' families, most of the pack is fast asleep, Melissa, Lars, and Lizzy included or so I think.

Tonight, something's different. The moment I close the apartment door, I hear a small, cranky voice pierce through the quiet apartment. Lars.

"Where's Pa?" he whines, his words wobbling with the frustration of a child who's waited too long. "You say we run when Pa get home. He nebber home!"

Ouch. The words hit me like a sucker punch to the gut. Worse than any I've taken in a fight. His little voice carries a weight I can't ignore. Guilt churns in my chest, and I hurry down the hall. When I peek into his room, the sight almost breaks me. Melissa sits beside him, trying to reassure him with her soft, soothing words. She's telling him that I *have* been home, just leaving before sunrise and coming back long after he's asleep. But even her voice sounds tired, tinged with sadness. She's had only fleeting kisses from me in passing, no real moments together as a family in days.

Tears sting my eyes as I take in the scene, guilt gnawing at me for every moment I've missed. I step into the room, my voice soft but steady. "Pa's home, buddy."

Lars' little face lights up, his frustration melting away as I scoop him into my arms. I press kisses into his messy black hair, holding him close as if to make up for all the lost time. Melissa watches us with a tired but warm smile, and I reach out, pulling her into the embrace. Our little family, except tiny Lizzy, wrapped together in a moment that feels all too fleeting. The weight of everything I've missed crashes over me. Lars and Lizzy were nearly taken from me before I even knew they existed. That thought ignites something inside me, a fierce determination to do better.

Alpha, I send through the mind-link, my tone firm but urgent. *I need to take tomorrow off.*

The response from Lenny comes through the mind-link: *Okay. Take the day. You've earned it.* Melissa looks up at me, surprise flashing in her tired eyes. Before she can say anything, I lean back to meet Lars' gaze. His big blue eyes are still watery, his lips quivering just a little.

"How about this, buddy?" I say, my voice lighter, trying to inject some hope into the room. "Pa and Ma will take the whole day off tomorrow. No work, no patrols, just us. We'll pack lunch, head to the woods, and spend the day together as a family. I'll have the patrol keep a section of the woods clear so you can shift and run to your heart's content and Lizzy can nap in nature. What do you think?"

His teary eyes widen, and for a moment, he looks uncertain, like he doesn't quite believe me. Then he nods, a slow, eager nod that makes my heart swell.

"Really?" His voice is a small, fragile thing, but I nod, my heart swelling.

Melissa squeezes my hand, her eyes shining with gratitude and love. Tomorrow won't erase all the long, exhausting days we've endured, but it's a start. As I tuck Lars into bed, I make a silent vow: no matter how chaotic things get, my family will always come first.

The next day, I watch my little pup dart and leap through the woods, his energy boundless and infectious. I run alongside him, feeling the ground beneath my feet and the wind rush past us, my senses alive with the forest's vibrance. Nearby, my mate, Melissa, sits in her human form, keeping a watchful eye on our sleeping she-pup, still too young to shift. The sight fills me with a deep sense of gratitude, and the weight of everything that's changed in just a few weeks hits me like a tidal wave.

So much has happened. So much has *changed.*

We found Lars, our nephew, no, our son now. He's a remarkable boy, extraordinary in ways that both amaze and worry me. His abilities make him special, yes, but they also make him a target. While Lars can hold his own in a fight, he's still a child who needs us, me and Mel, to shield him from the dangers that claws and teeth can't fend off. The council, humans, scientists... They'd see him as an experiment rather than a boy. They'd try to dissect his life, strip away his innocence, all because he shifted early and has powers they'll never understand. I almost lost him once. I won't let it happen again.

And then, there's Melissa. My beautiful, strong, compassionate mate. She's everything I ever dreamed of and more. Her wolf, Artemis, is as breathtaking as she is, fierce, nurturing, and perfectly named after the goddess of childbirth and the protector of children. A fitting name for Mel, my midwife mate, my partner, my love. She's not just perfect for me; she's perfect for Lars and Lizzy, too. Sweet, patient, and unyieldingly loyal. Five long years I waited for her. Five years she was just out of reach, studying at college, while I clung to the hope that someday I'd find the mystery girl that would be my forever. And now she's here, an irreplaceable part of our pack and our family.

But our family didn't stop there. Along with Lars came little Elizabeth, our baby girl. Lizzy. A tiny, perfect pup with bright eyes and a spirit that melts hearts. Lars saved her life when she was just moments old, and she's been adored by all of us ever since: me, Mel, Lars... even the alpha twins have taken a shine to her. The thought of her life being snuffed out before it even began chills me to the core. But she's here, alive and loved, and I'd lay down my life a thousand times over to keep it that way.

I went from having no family to a *full* family in the blink of an eye. My son, my mate, my daughter. My pack. My reason to fight.

And fight we did. We stood against evil and won. The war is over—at least for now. There's still work to do. We have to track down Bonfare and the pup Arioch, but that can wait. For today, for this moment, we rest.

I hear the soft crunch of leaves behind me and turn just in time to see my pup pounce. I let him catch me, of course. Like any good father, I roll with him, our play a blur of laughter and tussling. We wrestle, leap over fallen logs, and practice hiding in the underbrush, his little yips of excitement filling the air.

Eventually, Mel calls us over for lunch, her voice gentle but commanding. We gather around and eat together, the warmth of the moment settling deep into my soul. Afterward, we curl up in a pile, Lars nestled protectively in his wolf form beside Lizzy while Mel and I cuddle close with our pups tucked safely between us.

This is what I fought for. *This* is what makes it all worth it. Family. Pack. Happiness.

And I swear to myself, no matter what challenges come our way, I'll protect this—*them*—with everything I have.

Epilogue

Beta Jackson

"Pa!"

"Uncle Jax!"

"Uncle Jax!"

"Pa!"

"Uncle Jax!"

The moment I step onto the playground, I'm swarmed by three eight-year-old boys and two five-year-old girls. Their little arms latch onto me like I've been gone for weeks, even though yesterday's mission barely lasted overnight. Their laughter fills the air, high-pitched and wild, and for a moment, I let myself believe everything is as simple as their joy. But the truth is, I never stop searching.

I thought I'd found them this time: the two who slipped through my fingers all those years ago. Five years of silence, no word of kidnappings or attacks on packs, and yet I can't let it go. Not until every thread is tied, every shadow banished.

But right now, I'm home. It's family time.

I scoop up Lizzy, the smallest and most determined of the group, as she wraps her arms around my neck with a giggle. The others trail behind me like ducklings as I herd them inside, their excited chatter bouncing off the walls. First order of business: washing hands before lunch.

"Go on, you know the drill," I say, pointing them toward the sink. Lunch today is at the pack dining hall. It's not just about feeding hungry stomachs; it's about the bonds that keep us strong. Spending time with the pack is just as important as family time, and today, both worlds collide.

Our two families, mine and the Alpha's, share meals often. It's a tradition now, one that reminds us of what we've built together. The twins, Anthony and Alexander, still keep a watchful eye on Lizzy, as they always have. And Lars has his own reason for being protective of Paisley.

As we settle in, the usual routine unfolds. Lizzy and Paisley immediately swap chairs. Paisley, with her wide eyes and flushed cheeks, gravitates to the seat beside Lars, the Beta second child seat, where Lizzy should traditionally sit. She has what we all jokingly call a "puppy love" crush on her brothers' best friend. I can't help but think how amusing it is, knowing this small affection will become something real one day.

Lizzy, on the other hand, couldn't care less about crushes. She takes what should be Anthony's seat, right between him and Alexander. To her, sitting there means getting the best of both worlds, hanging out with her brother's friends and having Paisley, her best friend, just seats away. For her, life is about fun, games, and whatever mischief she and the boys can conjure up next.

Melissa and Luna Sara arrive next, their smiles warm and grounding as they join the table. Moments later, Alpha Lenny steps in, commanding the room without saying a word. As the meal begins, the familiar hum of conversation fills the air.

I glance around the table at the faces that mean the most to me, my family, pack, the people I'd lay down my life for without a second thought. Every meal together reminds me of why we fought, why we bled, and why we endured the horrors of war.

Piers Jameson and his rogue army are nothing but a bitter memory now. We destroyed that evil together, united and unyielding.

But today isn't about battles or the ghosts of the past. It's about this: Lizzy's laughter, Paisley's flushed cheeks when Lars teases her, the Alpha's booming laugh as Melissa tells a story.

Family and pack. That's what matters. That's what we protect.

Karin Davis, a medically retired firefighter paramedic, brings her dynamic energy to life in the vibrant San Francisco North Bay Area. A passionate fan of Star Wars, Disney, and Metallica, she dives into supernatural romance novels and thrills in Sci-fi and horror films. Karin shares her home with her soulmate, her talented teenager, and their two charismatic cats. As a dedicated band mom, she's often on the go, chauffeuring and chaperoning for her kid's band class. In her creative downtime, she crafts stunning multimedia art. Stay connected with Karin through her website and social media!

Website: www.monkeymommacreations.com
YouTube: @monkeymommacreations
https://monkeymommacreations.etsy.com
https://www.facebook.com/profile.php?id=1000
79166137913
amazon.com/author/karinmdavis